# THE FORTUNES OF TEXAS

*Follow the lives and loves of a complex family
with a rich history and deep ties
in the Lone Star State*

*HITTING THE JACKPOT*

The Maloneys of Chatelaine, Texas,
have just discovered they are blood relations
to the Fortunes—which makes them instant
millionaires. But their inheritance comes with
a big secret that could change everything
for their small-town family...

Alana Searle is holding out for a hero—a stable,
steady guy who's ready to settle down *and* raise
another man's baby. Coop Fortune Maloney
is a ranch hand with a reputation for fun and...
philandering. Alana is certain Coop can
never be the man she needs, but that doesn't stop
her from longing for something she can't have...

Dear Reader,

This is my first time working on The Fortunes of Texas series, so thank you for welcoming me into this wonderful Western world. The readers of this series are dedicated, loyal and amazing. You're the kind of reader I love to keep in mind as I develop a book.

I wanted to write about two people who've been in each other's circle for a while but were never free to be together. It turns out Alana Searle and Cooper Fortune Maloney are perfect for each other. They're both very much alike—out for a good time and plenty of laughs. The problem is Alana stopped laughing a few weeks ago. She's secretly pregnant by an ex-boyfriend who left as soon as he heard the news. In her situation, she naturally questions whether she'll have a real chance with Coop now that she's finally met her match.

If you've read this far, you can be assured there will be a happily-ever-after ending for these two, but getting there is half the fun!

I hope you enjoy reading Alana and Coop's romance as much as I did writing it. As always, I love to hear from you. You can reach me at heatherly@heatherlybell.com.

*Heatherly Bell*

# Winning
# Her Fortune

---

## HEATHERLY BELL

HARLEQUIN
**SPECIAL**
EDITION

Special thanks and acknowledgment are given to Heatherly Bell for her contribution to The Fortunes of Texas: Hitting the Jackpot miniseries.

Recycling programs for this product may not exist in your area.

ISBN-13: 978-1-335-72451-9

Winning Her Fortune

Harlequin Enterprises ULC
22 Adelaide St. West, 41st Floor
Toronto, Ontario M5H 4E3, Canada
www.Harlequin.com

Printed in U.S.A.

Bestselling author **Heatherly Bell** was born in Tuscaloosa, Alabama, but lost her accent by the time she was two. After leaving Alabama, Heatherly lived with her family in Puerto Rico and Maryland before being transplanted kicking and screaming to California's Bay Area. She now loves it here, she swears. Except the traffic.

### Books by Heatherly Bell

#### Harlequin Special Edition

##### *The Fortunes of Texas: Hitting the Jackpot*

*Winning Her Fortune*

##### *Charming, Texas*

*Winning Mr. Charming*
*The Charming Checklist*
*A Charming Christmas Arrangement*

##### *Montana Mavericks: The Real Cowboys of Bronco Heights*

*Grand-Prize Cowboy*

##### *Wildfire Ridge*

*More than One Night*
*Reluctant Hometown Hero*
*The Right Moment*

#### Harlequin Superromance

##### *Heroes of Fortune Valley*

*Breaking Emily's Rules*
*Airman to the Rescue*
*This Baby Business*

Visit the Author Profile page
at Harlequin.com for more titles.

For Vince Font, brother extraordinaire,
and the other writer in our family. Love you!

## *Prologue*

Here's something Cooper Fortune Maloney never thought he'd say: after tonight, he could add escort to his résumé. He waited for his time to go on the auction block. He removed his hat to run a hand through his hair, then dropped it back on, ready for his moment with the ladies.

It was Valentine's Day, and the night of the bachelor auction in Chatelaine, Texas. Tonight they were raising money for the Chatelaine Fish and Wildlife Conservation Society and two of his brothers were also participating.

Coop stood in the hot storage space where they'd put all the bachelors at the back of the Saddle & Spur Roadhouse. Bidding for his older brother Max had gone out of control. Lively and enthusiastic.

Just the way Coop liked things. Eliza Henry and Alana Searle were now battling it out for Max dollar by dollar. Everyone else had dropped out of the bidding.

Coop laughed as Max gave a tight smile and pulled at the collar of his shirt when Eliza once again outbid a frustrated Alana.

Coop had thought Max and Eliza were just friends. Since Max came into his Fortune silver mining inheritance, she was helping him find a house. Coop assumed she was just Max's Realtor. Now, she seemed to be giving Alana death glares every time she countered her bid.

Coop hoped Eliza's interest had nothing to do with the windfall Max had recently received. When Martin Smith had come to Chatelaine last month and handed his oldest brother, Lincoln, a check, all five of the Fortune Maloney children were given the shock of their lives. It turned out their grandfather Wendell Fortune had left a sizable inheritance from the silver and gold mines in Chatelaine. When his estate had tracked down his son, their father, Rick Maloney, they'd all learned of their father's death. That meant all his children would receive the inheritance. For some odd reason, Wendell's good friend Martin explained, the money was being disbursed slowly. So far, only Linc and Max had received their checks, Max just recently.

Coop looked at Max onstage, completely out

of his element. His brother hated anything that involved being the center of attention, but Cooper had jumped at the chance to have a little fun tonight. He didn't have a girlfriend at the moment and was free and clear of any romantic entanglements. Perfect. Whoever won him wasn't going to regret it for a second.

Eventually, Alana took a seat and didn't get up again, ending the bidding war. Coop figured they'd all have a good laugh later at how she'd pushed up the final price for Max.

"Aaaand sold to number fifty with the winning bid! Ladies, thank you for the enthusiastic bidding." The MC pointed to Alana and winked. "Especially the lady in red."

She was smoking hot in that short red dress with matching Western boots. With long blond hair and beautiful blue eyes, Alana had style. She was every man's type. Too bad for Max his Realtor won him instead.

Max walked to the back and met Coop. Quite frankly, he looked ridiculous dressed in the cowboy hat they were all wearing tonight. Max was an *accountant*, not a cowboy.

"I think Eliza must have a thing for you." Coop elbowed Max.

Eliza Henry was number fifty. The ladies were all bidding anonymously with numbered paddles, but Coop knew that Eliza Henry was Max's friend and Realtor. He didn't think anything else had been going on, but Eliza had been quite enthusiastic.

"She did me a favor. I asked her to make sure she got the winning bid for me. This is for charity, don't forget."

"All right, then. Whatever floats your boat," Coop said. "You better go meet your woman."

A bead of sweat slid down Max's face, and he pulled at his collar again. "Is it hot in here?"

"Yes. Good job bringing it, Mr. Hottie." Coop clapped his shoulder. "Eliza is a catch, which I'm sure you already know. Y'all have a good time tonight. Who knows? Maybe this is a chance to become more than friends."

"Yeah, yeah."

The way Coop understood things, tonight wasn't the actual date, just a short time to chat and get to know each other a little better. The other bachelor who'd already been auctioned had left the private room and was now near the restaurant section having a drink with the woman who'd won. Coop watched as Max awkwardly went to join Eliza and led her out of the room.

The youngest Fortune Maloney brother, Damon, came up behind Cooper. "Damn, did you see that? Alana Searle is bidding tonight. I would give anything for her to win me. I've had a crush on her *forever.*"

"Get in line. Who *doesn't* have a crush on her?

She's not interested in you. You saw what just happened. She wanted Max."

"So what?" Damon adjusted the cowboy hat he never wore. "I'm better-looking than Max, and I could be her consolation prize."

"Step aside, youngster, and let me show you how this is done." Coop walked toward the auctioneer's podium.

"Ladies, welcome our next bachelor, the notoriously single Cooper Fortune Maloney! Yes, that's right, ladies. He's one of the Fortunes of Texas. Let's hear it for this cowboy who promises you one wild ride!"

A gratifying swell of applause and whistles rose up over the room. Coop tipped his Stetson and flashed everyone a smile.

Vicky Chandler, an entertainment news reporter from Corpus Christi, was their MC tonight. She turned to Coop expectantly.

"Cooper, what kind of date do you promise the young lady who wins you tonight?"

He tipped back on his heels. "You'll have a good time. I'll make sure of it. We'll take a ride out to Lake Chatelaine and have a picnic, then watch the sun set. Whatever happens after, well, that will be ladies' choice. Let's just say I'm going to leave my entire night wide-open. We can stay up and watch the sunrise." He grinned. "I make a mean breakfast."

A few more whoops and hollers, and the auction began.

Within minutes, there were several bids from some excited women, and the price quickly increased. Some of his ex-girlfriends were bidding, which gave him pause. But hey, this was for charity. He'd go on a date with an ex if he had to, but he would prefer someone else to win. Someone like, for instance, Alana. *The lady in red.*

The bidding inched up, one lady always outbidding another. Then Alana reentered the room. He hadn't seen her in the crowd after she'd lost Max, probably having left to go lick her wounds. Now she raised her hand and made a bid several steps ahead of the last one.

This caused a general moan from the ladies, but Coop's ex-girlfriend Shannon rose to the challenge. When Alana jumped way ahead with her next bid, Shannon sat down in a huff.

"Aaaand sold, to number sixty-one. Congratulations. Way to hang in there." The MC pounded her gavel.

Coop walked toward Alana, who, if possible, looked even better close up. That dress was doing all kinds of things for him. She wore her blond hair down, her skin creamy and peachy, cheeks pinked. Probably from all the effort. Every time someone had outbid her tonight, she'd jumped up in her chair, springing up like a jack-in-the-box.

They'd gone to school together, like so many in

their small town, and so they were acquainted with each other. But she was four years younger, still in junior high when he'd been a senior. It had been out of the question for him then, as he had his own rules for dating. But beyond that, he'd always found her gorgeous and somewhat unattainable. Now, he wondered why they'd never dated after high school, since they seemed like a likely pairing. Both had reputations for hard partying and good times.

"How about that? I won the next-best brother," Alana said with a sly wink.

Coop winced, not from the raucous noise from the back room at the closing of the bidding on Damon, but from the reference to the "next-best" brother. But yeah, okay. He got it. At the moment, since his inheritance hadn't come in, he supposed one *could* look at it that way.

Then again, he'd always had more game than Max.

"I'm kidding!" She elbowed him.

"Don't worry, darlin', I'll make sure you don't ever regret winning *me*." He sent her his most wicked smile.

"I'm sure I won't."

"Would you like to get a drink, and we can talk about this date I'm taking you on?" He pointed her toward the bar.

"Um, sure."

When they each took a stool, he ordered a beer, but Alana wanted a soft drink.

"Not drinking tonight?" Coop handed her the soda.

"Everyone asks me that." She didn't meet his eyes. "It's…this new diet I'm on."

*Diet?* What kind of diet allowed a sugared soft drink but no alcohol? What the hell did he know. He'd never dieted a day in his life.

"Thanks for outbidding Shannon. We dated once a while ago, and let's just say I didn't want to go there again." He took a pull of his beer. "So, tell me, what do you like to do on a date?"

"Probably some of the same things you do." She smiled—if he wasn't mistaken, a bit wickedly.

The rumors swirling around flirty Alana were apparently true. She was aggressive and knew who and what she wanted. Once again, two of a kind. He could play that game. It sounded like they were very much in sync, at least in one way. Coop couldn't wait to find out more.

"Well." He waggled his brows. "That kind of thing could take me all night."

"Promise?"

Damn, Coop really liked this girl. He would schedule this date tomorrow if possible.

"You got it, sweetheart. I'm your man."

She shook her head. "Don't say that. I know you would have never asked me out on your own."

This was probably true, but only because she hadn't been on his radar recently. She'd worked at GreatStore with Linc, until he'd received his inheritance and quit. And she'd been dating Patrick, a fellow ranch hand. Every time Coop saw Alana, in fact, she'd been with some guy.

Until tonight.

"You date a lot," he explained. "I didn't think I stood a chance."

"I could say the same thing about you, cowboy."

This was true, so he didn't bother arguing. "Well, I think you're beautiful."

"Thank you, that's sweet."

"It's the truth." He leaned forward. "So, what did you have in mind for this date that will probably last all night long?"

She sipped from her soft drink and gazed at him from hooded eyelids. "Surprise me."

Yet one more thing they had in common. She liked surprises.

"Just wait. It's going to be epic."

# Chapter One

*The Chatelaine Report: We are still feeling the ripple effects from last month's Valentine's Day Bachelor Auction. Max Maloney Fortune is now engaged to real estate agent Eliza Henry, who "won" Max on Valentine's Day. We particularly admired the determination of Alana Searle, who landed Max's brother Coop as a consolation prize. Look out, Chatelaine! There's no telling what might happen when two of the town's most colorful characters wind up together...*

*One month later*

Alana Searle might've won Cooper Fortune Maloney at the Valentine's Day Bachelor Auction, but she should probably give him back.

The auction had been for charity, and Alana figured spending the birthday money Nana sent her every year would be a good "pay it forward" gesture. Besides, Nana always made her promise to spend the money on "something special" for herself and not on paying her many bills. This was the perfect situation, because when else could she give money to charity and still get something for herself? She'd tried to win Max, but the bidding had quickly gone out of her range.

Of all four Fortune Maloney brothers, Coop was by far the best-looking in her opinion. Tall and lean, with strong arms and muscular thighs, he was a feast for any woman's eyes. He had dark bedroom eyes that she'd wager regularly saw the inside of a woman's room. His wavy brown hair was always tousled by the wind, and he usually appeared to have recently dismounted a horse.

A studly cowboy through and through.

Unfortunately, there was a word for men like him. *Player* was the nicest. Women tended to lick their lips and toss their hair when Coop walked by. Once upon a time, she'd been one of them. And oh yes, he noticed the attention he got. A huge flirt, he always had a kind word for the ladies. Those words involved "sweetheart" and "darlin'" even to women he didn't know.

He was precisely the type of man who should stay at least a hundred miles away from Alana. He was trouble. And she already had enough trouble of her own, thank you. But he'd been her consolation prize at the bachelor auction, and she wasn't too jaded to give Cooper a chance tonight. After all, he was one of the Fortune Maloneys, one sister and four brothers of solid character and strength. His brother Lincoln had been the best boss Alana ever had. Lincoln hadn't changed who he was after his inheritance made him a wealthy man. Now, he was in a serious relationship with Remi Reynolds, one of Alana's good friends and a former coworker. Alana couldn't be happier for them both.

Maybe Cooper could surprise her tonight. There might be a lot more depth to this cowboy than anyone realized. The same could be said of her, after all. Some people in town didn't hold the best opinions of her, either. She wanted to be fair and give him the benefit of the doubt. He'd kept calling to schedule their date, but there was always a conflict either on his side or hers. Four weeks later, the day had finally arrived.

Tonight might be the last time she'd get to go out for a little fun before everyone in their small town of Chatelaine discovered her little secret, so she'd talked herself into enjoying the evening. She would make it a quick night, however, and insist he bring her home early, making up some excuse about work.

Though the Valentine's Day auction had been for

a good cause, she'd lost her head when she'd been outbid on her intended bachelor. Coop's brother Max was handsome, too, plus he was stable and secure. He'd been her first choice. Max managed an accounting firm, for crying out loud. Did it get any safer than that? Rumors in town were that Max was a commitment-phobe, but she'd hoped maybe his being older than Coop, he might be ready to have a family and settle down. Alana had his ready-made family waiting for him right here, but no dice. She lost the auction to an incredibly zealous Eliza, who'd obviously had a bigger budget than Alana. Eliza and Max were together now—full confirmation that despite being anti-commitment, Max had become serious with a woman once he found the right one.

While plenty of women were upset that Alana had made the winning bid for Cooper, she imagined those women only wanted a fun night out. The man might as well have a sign around his neck that read Call Coop for a Good Time. She'd flirted mercilessly with him that night, too, still on a high at having actually won a Fortune Maloney brother. But a month had passed, which brought a lot of physical changes for her.

Alana didn't want a good time anymore, or a hot cowboy looking for some fun. She lowered her hand to her belly. Someone tiny and innocent depended on her, and she would not let him or her down. It was time to be smart. Time to find a man with character who would stand by her when he learned she was pregnant with another man's child. Not an easy task.

Starting off life without a father was not what she wanted for her little one. Not that she'd planned on any of this. Another cowboy had spoken sweet words she'd wanted to believe and taken her to bed. She'd thought she'd started something permanent and lasting with Patrick O'Shaughnessy, because she wasn't the girl most people in town believed her to be. Her reputation far exceeded her experience. There was a time when she'd been wild, back in high school, a long time ago now. All she'd ever wanted was someone to love. But men didn't love her, no matter how hard she tried. They wanted to sleep with her and eventually move on.

When Patrick learned she was pregnant, he'd practically left a cartoonlike shape of his body in the wall when he ran. She hadn't seen him since.

Yeah. Handsome cowboys were nothing but trouble.

She'd wanted someone solid and reliable, like Lincoln or Max. The brothers were all stand-up guys. She'd dated Lincoln once a while ago, but there had been no spark. He'd been a good guy and hadn't taken advantage of her willingness at the time. He was a good boss, and a good man, but he didn't exactly make her want to rip her clothes off.

No chemistry. Same with Max. She'd been around him enough to realize he was predictable, steady and safe. And while she didn't feel any zip or zing, surely that would have grown with time.

But Coop? He was dangerously attractive. And she had to be *done* with bad boys.

The doorbell rang, and trouble stood on the other side of it. Waiting. She sighed, grabbed her purse and threw open the door.

"Hey, Coop."

"Hiya, darlin'. Lord, you look beautiful tonight. You ready for this?" He grinned and tipped his hat.

Oh, yeah, he had dimples. A cleft in his chin. Super. This guy couldn't be any better-looking if he tried.

She shut and locked the front door before he got any ideas about coming inside. While in Coop's presence, she planned to stay as far away from a bedroom as possible. She didn't trust her often-impulsive nature, especially when it came to hotter-than-a-three-alarm-fire cowboys.

"Thanks for picking me up."

"Well, of course. My mama raised me right." He offered her his elbow.

She tucked her arm through his, sensing this to be a safe-enough activity. "Where are you taking me?"

"An old-fashioned picnic by the lake. What do you say?"

"I won you in an auction, Coop, I'm going on a date with you no matter where you take me."

He held the passenger door open to his weathered sky blue pickup truck. "You'll have a good time, I promise."

She froze and met his eyes. It was important to clarify something. On the night of the auction, she might have given him a different impression. She recalled some pretty heavy flirting on both their sides.

"Oh, I'm not interested in a good time."

"Why?" He blinked. "You want to have a bad time?"

"I think you know what I mean." She climbed into the truck, refusing his outstretched hand, and he shut the door, slowly shaking his head.

Coop drove them to Lake Chatelaine on the outskirts of town, to the public area designated for townies such as herself. Cooper didn't belong to the elite LC crowd, either, although she imagined soon, like his older brothers, Lincoln and Max, he'd have enough money to pay for a membership to the lake's fancy LC Club. There he could hang out with Lincoln, Max and all the other multimillionaires.

"Look." Alana pointed as they arrived and parked. In the distance was the sprawling LC Club, a stone structure that combined rustic flair with old-world elegance. Its numerous balconies overlooked the best parts of the lake. "There's your future."

He squinted in the direction and cocked his head. "Not *my* future."

Maybe he felt this way because the LC Club mostly catered to the wealthy from out of town. "Why not? You'll have plenty of money soon enough."

"I prefer to spend my time on a ranch with the horses." He reached into the back seat to grab a straw picnic basket. "Any day of the week."

She climbed out before he could open the door for her. Even so, he still took her hand and led her to a spot with a lovely view of the lake.

"I like to watch the sunset from right here," he said.

He spread the blanket under a tree. The lingering and waning daylight dappled through the wide branches of the old sycamore.

No doubt he enjoyed the view, and she'd bet never alone.

"Did you bring me to your favorite make-out spot?" she teased.

"What?" He pointed to himself in mock outrage. "Me? I would never."

"Oh, yes, you would." She couldn't help but smile.

He looked gorgeous and sexy in his dark jeans, pearl-button top, Stetson and cowboy boots. This was one delicious cowboy. He looked both tasty and sweet, and she might as well be a diabetic.

"Help yourself." He opened the top to the basket and offered her a cold soda.

He'd remembered that she wasn't drinking alcohol, which was nice, too, but she wondered how he'd feel if he knew the real reason.

She knelt on the edge of the blanket and accepted the drink. "Thanks."

He eyed her sitting as far away from him as possible and chuckled. "Do I scare you or something?"

"Ha! Don't be ridiculous."

He didn't need to frighten her. She was doing that all by herself.

She went ahead and crawled to the center of the blanket next to him while he pulled out several store-bought cartons. There were containers of macaroni salad, potato salad, broccoli salad, fried chicken and finger sandwiches. She recognized them from the deli counter at GreatStore, where she worked—they were some of their bestselling items. Thank goodness he'd ignored any of her fake diet restrictions here. Either that or he was a typical guy who didn't know or care about the calorie content of most foods.

"Thought you might enjoy an old-fashioned kind of date. You look like a sweet and wholesome girl to me."

She nearly choked on her soda and swallowed carefully. *No one* saw her that way.

"I do?"

"Why? Does that surprise you?"

"Well, yeah." She shrugged, not wanting to bring

up the ugly and painful rumors. "But thanks for saying that."

A kind sentiment, after all, and she relaxed a little and helped herself to some macaroni salad.

If Coop believed this about her, then he probably had no ideas of getting further than hand-holding tonight.

Coop stretched out on the picnic blanket next to Alana and took another bite of the chicken drumstick. She was right. Soon his entire life would change. Now that both Linc and Max had received their Fortune inheritance, it hopefully wouldn't be long before he'd get his.

Not long ago a man named Martin Smith had made a shocking revelation to Coop's family. They had all gathered together in Rambling Rose for the celebration of his sister Justine's wedding to Stefan Mendoza. There, they had been informed by Martin that their father, Rick Maloney, was actually the illegitimate son of Wendell Fortune.

He was the multimillionaire who'd owned the silver mines in Chatelaine. If that in itself wasn't enough of a surprise, Martin—who'd explained that he was once the late Wendell's best friend—then told them that Wendell's will left everything to his only surviving progeny. All five of the Maloney grandchildren. They would soon all be given their inheritance. So far, only Lincoln and Max had received theirs but all five of them were expected to receive a check.

Despite what Alana suggested, however, Coop couldn't see himself as a member of the elite LC Club. Not in a million years. God and nature had created this lake, and everyone should enjoy its beauty. One could do it from a picnic blanket like they were or from those high-rise balconies. It was the same lake one way or the other.

But he didn't entirely disagree with Alana's point. His life would change with the kind of money he'd receive. His rightful inheritance from the silver mines discovered by his grandfather Wendell Fortune would arrive for him soon. Martin claimed it was held up due to a technicality. But once it arrived, Coop didn't ever see himself hanging out with a bunch of hoity-toity rich folks.

His plans so far were to have huge weeklong parties for all his friends and buy a tricked-out new truck. A Land Rover. Hell, maybe two of them. One and a spare, kind of like a king. He'd then buy a cattle ranch and hire others to be his ranch hands. He'd pay them a fair wage, too, because since he'd worked on a ranch, he knew the work would break anyone's back some days. Nothing *he* couldn't handle.

"What made you agree to do the bachelor auction?" Alana asked. "I know Max wasn't too excited about it. He had to be roped into it."

He shrugged. "Sounded like fun. I'm usually up for anything."

"Yeah, I heard that about you." She snorted.

"Really? What have you heard?"

"Nothing." She shook her head slowly, fighting a smile.

He didn't understand Alana, and he was fairly intuitive when it came to women. At least, he'd always thought so. Up until now, he hadn't had money or prospects, and he drove a very old truck. But he'd still had plenty of interest from women. When he'd heard about the Valentine's Day Bachelor Auction, his first thought was *why not?* It was for a good cause, and he loved women. He considered himself lucky to have been won by Alana. The moment she had the highest bid, he wanted to close the auction himself and just yell, "Sold to the beautiful blonde in the back!"

"You used to go out with Patrick, didn't you?" He wasn't close with the guy, but as a fellow cowboy in their small town, they'd crossed paths a time or two.

"We broke up."

"Figured, or he'd want to have me killed for going on a date with you. I haven't run into him for a while."

"He left town. Moved."

When he quirked a brow with an unspoken question, she shrugged.

"I have no idea where or why. So, what are you going to do with all the money you inherit?"

It was an abrupt shift in topic, and he noticed her reluctance to talk about Patrick. That was fine with Coop. He wanted her to forget the guy ever existed.

"Probably something wild and impulsive, if I know me. It's better that I don't have the money right away. I'd probably blow it too soon."

"Doing what?"

"A huge seven-day party in Las Vegas, for starters. What happens in Vegas stays in Vegas, so I won't answer to anyone. Then maybe Cancún for a week—fly all my friends and family out. I'd rent a mansion right on the water. One of those where the pool practically meets the ocean. Surfing, snorkeling, dancing, drinking and hanging out and having a good time." He turned to her, expecting a pleasant expression. "How does that sound?"

Far from a smile, she looked like she'd just received bad news. "I guess it sounds like fun."

"Really? Then why do you look depressed? You can come, too, of course."

She chuckled. "No, I can't, but thanks for the invite."

Curious, because he hadn't even mentioned a firm date. After all, he had no idea when his windfall would come. The way she'd initially sat so far from him, and the way she avoided his eyes, made him wonder whether she liked him at all.

"Okay, well. If you change your mind." He lay back on the blanket, crossing his arms behind his neck.

"I won't. You know, I used to be a lot more like you."

Those words intrigued him, and he wondered what she meant. She was still young and single. Gorgeous, a tiny thing compared to his six-foot-plus height, with pale blond hair and nearly translucent peachy skin. She always dressed well, probably because she got employee discounts at GreatStore. Today she wore a short white dress displaying some of the best legs he'd ever seen. Long, and creamy, he imagined they would be soft and silky to his touch. She wore a light denim jacket and Western boots with brown-and-blue tooling.

Who or what was stopping *her* from having a little fun?

"Why have you changed?"

"We all have to grow up sometime." She took a bite of a coconut macaroon and stared out to where a duck had alighted on the lake, then took off, its wings splashing.

"Why would you want to do that?" Coop laughed, trying to lighten the mood. "Adulting isn't any fun."

"It's not too bad once you have a real reason. Like an..." She seemed to consider her words carefully. "Anchor."

"An *anchor*? Sweetheart, an anchor holds you down."

This time, she met his eyes. "It also keeps a ship from drifting off course."

"Yeah, but you're not a boat. And why would you want anyone or anything holding you back and keeping you from moving forward?"

"That's only one way of looking at it. The other way is that an anchor is safety and stability. And I need that right now."

He didn't want to argue the point. From time to time, he wondered if all the money he'd receive would hold him back in some way. Sometimes he worried becoming a multimillionaire meant he'd have to change who he was, who he hung out with and what he did with his time. He'd almost certainly have to be a little more cautious with women and didn't relish the idea.

Well, whether she wanted it or not, the idea of the anchor she'd referred to didn't make her happy, from what he could tell.

Never let it be said a woman left his company without a smile. He would need to work a little harder tonight.

Most of the women he dated would be all over him by now, kissing and grabbing, ready for some action. Not to brag, but yeah, women seemed to find him good-looking enough. Well, maybe not Alana. That was okay with him. He had no idea or hope to sleep with her tonight. He simply wanted to enjoy a relaxing evening with a beautiful woman who had never been available to him in the past.

Too bad this auction hadn't happened after he had some serious coin to spend. But a man didn't need to romance a woman with caviar and champagne. For now, he'd improvise. Maybe someday he'd look back with fondness on these times when he had no money. It was a funny thought, because he'd always managed just fine with what he had.

As they ate, the sun slid down the horizon in bright, splashy curls of pink and purple. By the time they were finished, they were engulfed in the darkness, the only light coming from the gleam of a half-moon as it reflected off the lake.

Coop stood, brushed off his legs and used his phone to light his way toward his truck. "I'll be right back. Don't you go anywhere."

"Actually, I was thinking I should go home soon. I have to work tomorrow."

"Nah. You'll want to get as much mileage out of me as possible on this date. You paid good money for me." He reached inside the lowered driver's side window, inserted his key and turned on his headlights.

Then he tuned in the local country music station.

"That's going to drain your battery." Alana stood. "I have some music on my phone if that's what you want."

"Service isn't great out here." He offered his out-stretched hand. "Do you want to dance?"

"Here?" She blinked and tossed her hair. "Now?"

"What else are you doing?"

"Um, well…okay."

It had been a while since he'd done this, too, cut loose dancing in the dark, the headlights of his truck beaming, music droning from his junky speakers.

He'd always found it fun to dance outside in the dark. Dance halls were okay, too, but there was something about the outdoors that made Coop come alive. But right now, standing in front of this beautiful woman, Coop was nervous for the first time since he could recall.

His instinct was to pull her close, one hand on her waist and one on her hip. But something about Alana said, "keep your hands to yourself." Which was strange to him, given her enthusiasm on the night of the auction. He wasn't one to push the issue if a woman wasn't interested in getting close.

She wasn't dating anyone else, and the anchor talk sure made her sound ready to settle down. And that itself might be the problem. She read this cowboy right. He didn't appreciate the idea of an anchor holding him back. But previously, Alana had been the same way.

Not anymore.

Something had definitely changed.

## Chapter Two

The last time Coop danced this way he'd been alone. It had been nighttime, dark and storming when he'd driven out to the lake on his way back from Rambling Rose. Earlier that day he'd been told by his grandfather's old friend and partner, Martin, that he and his siblings all had a substantial inheritance coming to them. Because of the silver mines—and apparently a gold mine, too!—their grandfather had co-owned, after his death, they would all be multimillionaires. All were Fortunes, if not officially by name, then by heritage.

He'd driven out to the lake after receiving the life-changing news, kept his headlights on, yelled, jumped for joy and danced in the rain.

Now, as "Boot Scootin' Boogie" played, Coop continued to swing dance with Alana. She knew all the steps and easily kept up with him. And he got her to smile.

"Don't you step on my foot! These boots are brand-new and I saved up months for them."

"They're nice." He lowered his gaze. "I won't step on you, long as you don't step on me."

She laughed. "You're so big and tall, if I step on your foot, I doubt you'll notice."

"Oh, I'll notice."

If only because if he got her close enough to step on his foot, well, let's just say he'd be a happy man.

Right now, they were dancing approximately an arm's length away from each other. He had a bit of a reputation for being bold, so what the heck, he went ahead and indulged in his recent history. He pulled Alana close to him on one of the turns, and she gazed up at him, her eyes shimmering, a hint of a smile on her full lips. The top lip was slightly larger than the bottom, giving her an almost puckered and ready-for-a-kiss look.

*Lord, she's gorgeous.*

He'd been with plenty of pretty women, but there was something about Alana. She stoked a fire deep inside him. It seemed like she knew him, and far *too* well, as if maybe she could see inside him. Tonight, she'd helped to remind him that no matter how much money he'd eventually have, nights like these would always be part of his agenda. Right along with a down-to-earth woman who'd appreciate the little things in life.

They danced to three songs in a row, both laughing, her slightly breathless. Then a slower tune came on, Sam Hunt's "Make You Miss Me." Only, Sam Hunt performed songs no one had any idea how to dance to. Coop chose to slow things down and pulled Alana even closer. Her hair smelled like the pink flowers in his mother's front yard.

"I like this song," Coop said, because he had no idea what else to say.

This actually wasn't his favorite song by the artist. The lyrics were about a man trying to get over a woman who'd broken his heart. A little depressing, come to think of it.

"I love Sam Hunt," Alana said. "He tells it like it is."

"But if we're thinking of our first song, we might have to go with 'Boot Scootin' Boogie.' This one is a little sad. Cheer up, Sam. It can't be all that bad."

"Coop!" Alana laughed. "Don't make fun of Sam's heartache."

He winced. "I'm sorry. I hate songs where people are feeling sorry for themselves."

"He doesn't feel *sorry* for himself. He's simply

trying to get his girl back. Reminding her he's not going to be easy to forget."

"You obviously understand the song better than I do."

The song ended too soon, and the DJ came on with a stupid commercial, disrupting the mood. They simply stared at each other for a long moment, fingers and hands still entwined.

Alana disengaged first and lightly flattened her small hand against his chest. "I really do have to get home now. Thank you for a great dinner. You're a lot of fun, and I'm glad I won you."

"Instead of Max?" He winked, because he'd noticed her enthusiastic bidding on his older brother, too, and losing to Eliza. "Who knows? That could have been you, happily dating my big brother. Which would have been bad luck for me."

She blinked and shook her head. "No, those two are perfect for each other. I didn't see it then, but Eliza is the perfect woman for Max. I'm glad she outbid me."

"Happy to be your consolation prize."

"Hardly. You're the prize, Coop, and don't let anyone tell you otherwise."

Gratified, he grabbed the picnic basket with a grin. She picked up the blanket and walked with him to the truck.

Coop drove slowly back to town, wanting every

spare minute left to just enjoy talking to Alana on this crisp, clear night. They chatted about her job at GreatStore. She was what they called a floater, filling in different departments as needed, but she preferred working in women's wear. He told her about his work as a ranch hand and his passion for horses. When he pulled up at her home, naturally, he walked her to the front door. An awkward time for most, but not for Coop. He read signals with the speed of an air traffic controller.

She had allowed him to hold her hand to the front door, and when he caught her staring at his lips, he was encouraged enough to lean in. Alana closed the small distance, and they kissed. Not a sweet kiss, as he might have expected, but a deep and soulful one.

He'd never felt this kind of desperate need for someone, this pulling and tugging at him that he wanted more. That he might never get enough. Sinking fingers into her hair, he held her so she wouldn't think of getting away from him. He heard a soft moan from her and deepened the kiss.

He was fully aware he'd started this, but she did not pull away from him for several amazing seconds.

"Thank you again for a wonderful night."

"Can I see you again?" he blurted out like a love-sick teenager.

*Where did that come from?* Normally, he waited

a day or two to call for another date. A time-out. A breather to wait it out and see if he really missed the woman enough to ask for a second date.

And here he stood practically begging to see her again.

"I don't think so. We shouldn't waste each other's time. I'm not the right girl for you."

He was still holding her hand, so he squeezed it. "Why not?"

"Just…believe me. Take my word for it."

How did he get it so wrong? Was she playing hard to get? This was definitely not the reputation she had. She was supposed to be a good time, and he wanted some fun tonight. With her and not anyone else. The surprising desire he felt for her made his heart race, but he had too much pride to ask twice. She'd made her decision and he would respect that.

Confused by all her mixed signals, he let go of her hand. "All right."

"But whoever she is, she's going to be the luckiest woman in the world. You're a good guy."

He did not feel like an angel right now, his thoughts going to some sensual places after that hot kiss.

"Um, thanks. I had fun, too."

Then she smiled once more and went inside, leaving him on her porch. Alone.

Not a position he was used to.

\* \* \*

Alana braced her back against the door after shutting it closed, an internal battle raging. She waited for Cooper to leave, and after a few seconds, she heard his truck start and drive off. Only then could she relax, because it was too late to swing the door wide-open and say, *I was just kidding! Come inside and let's fool around. After all, I can't get any more pregnant than I already am.*

But no, she was going to do better now. Behave herself around men wanting to knock boots with her and not much else. This month, she'd crossed into her second trimester and had begun to show. She wasn't obvious to everyone and worked hard to disguise her swollen belly with her outfits. But anyone who saw her naked would know in a heartbeat. Her middle had thickened considerably, making her look like she'd gained weight, but only around the waist.

Who was she kidding? Her breasts were larger, too, swollen and painful to the touch. She'd have to buy a larger size soon, as well as start wearing clothes with elastic.

She undressed and pulled on her roomy sweats and T-shirt, then went to the freezer for her ice cream stash. What the heck. If she was going to get fat anyway, she might as well enjoy this. Putting some cherry vanilla in a bowl for courage, she decided tonight would be the night she'd tell her parents. Because nothing could ruin this feeling, not even telling her parents that their only daughter would be a single mom. She was still flying high from a wonderful evening with a gorgeous man.

And the kiss… Wow, the *kiss*. Cooper sure knew how to make a woman feel alive with his amazing mouth. He took possession, knew exactly what he was doing, and she'd had all kinds of tingles from a single touch. He'd put his entire body and soul into that kiss. Too bad this auction hadn't come around last year, before she'd started dating Patrick. She'd just never imagined that someone like Cooper Maloney would be interested in *her*.

As teenagers, they'd skirted around each other, Coop four years older. Though she had the interest of plenty of senior classmen that year in their small school, Coop never even gave her a second glance. He always had a girlfriend hanging on his every word, and she'd never stood a chance at getting to know him better.

Tonight, he'd given her every signal he'd wanted another date, even before he'd literally asked. But she'd given him the chance she promised herself she would, and tingles be damned, he *hadn't* changed. He wanted to have parties, blow his money and celebrate his wealth with his friends. And he had every right to do that.

Once, she might have done the same. But she

wasn't lying when she'd told him about her anchor. All she'd left out was its name. She already loved her baby more than she'd ever thought possible. At last month's ultrasound, she'd listened to the heartbeat and literally seen her baby's profile. Amazing and breathtaking. A precious new life for which she alone would be responsible.

She'd accepted everything would change and now looked forward to the baby.

The moment after she'd seen the second line appear on the early home pregnancy test, she'd promptly thrown up. Not because of any morning sickness, but because she was terrified. This had not been in the plans.

Even before she'd told Patrick, she'd suspected he wouldn't take it well. He was all about a good time, and they'd both been careful not to complicate their lives with an unplanned pregnancy. It happened anyway when the condom broke.

The pregnancy had come as a surprise to both of them, but only one of them walked away. She wondered if Patrick's feelings would have changed if he'd had a chance to listen to their baby's heartbeat the way she had.

So, she didn't have Patrick and she'd be a single mom even though the thought of the struggles she might have continued to fill her with anxiety.

But that didn't mean she wanted to drag anyone

else along who clearly wasn't ready. That was Coop, without a doubt. He still had many hell-raising days ahead of him. She couldn't trust him to be the man of character and strength she would need by her side.

Alana took one fortifying spoonful of ice cream, the sweet, heavy cream feeling like a hug from an old friend. Then she settled down on the couch and phoned her mother.

"Hi, sweetheart!" Mom said happily. "Daddy and I were just on our way out the door. Date night."

"Oh, well, don't let me keep you."

Alana pretended she hadn't called on this very day and hour knowing they were creatures of habit who had a date every Friday night at this time. One could set their clock by those two. She really wanted to tell her mother she was knocked up. Honestly. It just…wasn't going to be easy.

Her parents had the kind of enviable twenty-eight-year marriage most people would give their right heart ventricle for. They'd always been close and so deeply in love that Alana had sometimes felt like an intruder in their happy little union. Her mother was called "baby," so Alana was simply called "honey" as an endearment, and "Al" for a nickname. As a teenager, Alana was envied by all her friends. She got away with everything since her parents were so preoccupied with each other.

Alana was interested in sex far earlier than any

of her friends. She snuck out of the house when her parents had gone to bed and went to find her own fun. Often this involved heavy make-out sessions with her current boyfriend which went further than what she'd been ready for. Then she'd lost her virginity at age sixteen with the boy she believed to be the love of her life.

That was the year she discovered most boys didn't think sex meant love.

Unfortunately, that also meant she'd also developed a bit of a reputation among her peers. But though she'd been wild and carefree, all that changed a few years ago. The rumors of her active love life were mostly untrue. Now, she never slept with a guy before the third date. Even so, her dating life involved men who never stuck around much past that third date.

She realized her parents' marriage was one to envy and emulate, but she thought they could have done a lot of things differently, too. If she'd had more attention from them, maybe she wouldn't have been seeking it from boys when she'd been far too young.

"Don't be silly," her mom said now. "We have a few minutes. How are you?"

"Um, well, I wanted to…tell you I'm…"

Dear God, why was this so difficult?

"Yes?"

"I—I want to come visit soon."

Several years ago, her parents had sold the home she'd grown up in and moved from Chatelaine, Texas, to San Diego, California. Dad had a very attractive employment offer there, so they'd made the move. They'd invited Alana along, of course, mostly out of the kindness of their hearts, she suspected. They were undoubtedly relieved when she felt ready, at eighteen, to be on her own. And she hadn't wanted to leave any of her friends behind, so she'd stayed in Chatelaine. She and her best friend, Lucy, had rented a house together.

This year, Lucy would be celebrating her fourth wedding anniversary and was pregnant with her second child. All her friends were now married and doing those couple-centric things together. Like having babies. Alana always thought she'd be married by now, too, but it had never happened. Not with any of her high school boyfriends, and not with the few boyfriends she'd had after.

Like her friends, Alana wanted a husband and babies. The whole white picket fence. She still liked and enjoyed sex but since Patrick she was now more guarded of the men she chose. Lucy regularly reminded her that if she wanted marriage, she'd have to hold the sex away as a kind of carrot stick. That was when she'd come up with the whole three-date rule.

Somewhere in Chatelaine there had to be the right man for her.

Contrary to rumors, she didn't have a long list of lovers. People assumed so, maybe because of the way she dressed, her past and her still-flirty attitude. And probably because of the fact she remained single. Now she would probably cement everyone's belief in her lifestyle, too, the moment they discovered her secret.

Not only was she pregnant, but by a deadbeat who'd left town when she gave him the news. Mom had talked to Alana about birth control early on, and frequently. She knew better. There was no excuse, but accidents happened, and the pill always made her sick. She practiced safe and responsible sex, but obviously that hadn't been enough.

She bit her lower lip and tried to work up the courage to tell her mother.

*I want to come and visit because I need to tell you I'm having a baby.*

"Oh, that would be so wonderful," Mom said, then called to Alana's dad. "Babe, Alana wants to come visit us soon."

"The guest room is ready for you," he yelled back.

"You haven't visited since Christmas, so this will be wonderful."

Yeah, not so wonderful. They'd be disappointed when they found out Alana had messed up her life.

She was supposed to be furthering her education. Her parents didn't seem to think she could be happy working at GreatStore forever. But she loved it there and got along with all her coworkers. The store employed most of their small-town residents, and everyone else was either a rancher or in business for themselves. This was life in a small rural town, and her parents seemed to have already forgotten.

"Okay, Mom. I'll let you go. Give Dad a kiss for me."

"Wait. When do you think you'll come?"

"I don't know. Definitely soon." What was that about not being able to travel in the last trimester? She had another trimester to go. "I'll need to put in for a few days off."

"Let me know when you've finalized your plans. We'll buy the plane ticket."

"I'll let you know." Alana hung up and licked the ice cream bowl clean.

*Strike one. Two more swings before I'm out.*

She'd tell them as soon as she figured out how to do it without giving them matching heart attacks.

A few days later, Alana was stocking the new designer line of bras and panties in the ladies' lingerie department. Ever since Cooper dropped her off after their date and she'd spoken to her parents, she'd made a firm decision. A big one. She couldn't keep this pregnancy secret much longer and wanted

*someone* to talk to. Someone who would understand
and be supportive. Lucy would judge and remind
her she should have stopped being such a flirt long
ago. Remind her that she always seemed to pick the
wrong men. Guys who were fun and handsome but
lacked character. Her friend Remi would be worried, and would no doubt tell Lincoln, who would
then tell her boss before Alana was ready for Paul
Scott to know. There seemed to be only one person
who would truly understand her position, because
she was in the same boat.

When it was time for her break, she walked over
to see her coworker Sari, who was in the women's
wear department tagging clearance items. She was
new to GreatStore, having started work a few weeks
ago. So far, Alana could already see she was a hard
worker.

"Hey," Alana said. "How was your day off?"

*"Day off?* What is this thing you speak of? I
don't know what a day off is, or what it looks like,"
she joked.

Sari Keeling was the mother of two young
children. Unfortunately, she was also a widow at
only thirty-five years old. Even if life had sucker
punched her, she inspired Alana daily with her positive attitude.

"What *did* you *do* yesterday?" Alana reframed
the question.

"Benjy had a soccer game, and it was my turn

to bring snacks. Then Jacob started throwing up on the way home, which warranted a little diversion to Urgent Care. Poor little guy, but he's fine, probably just ate too many sliced oranges. We had dinner from the drive-through for the first time in years, because apparently, I'm not perfect. Later, we rented a movie as a special treat. A kids' movie, of course. I haven't seen an adult movie in years. I ended the day sleeping between two little ones and slept so hard I didn't even hear my alarm go off this morning. Honestly, I almost look forward to 'work.'" She held up air quotes. "I don't work nearly as hard as I do on my day off, and I get to speak to adults and everything."

Alana had spent enough time talking to Sari in the employees' locker room to understand. The life of a single mom wasn't a sheer delight. She'd been warned.

Like Sari, she'd have to get used to doing it all herself. Alana didn't have anyone to call or go with her, either, if her baby got sick and needed a trip to Urgent Care. And what if something was wrong with her baby, what on earth would she do then? There were so many fears, both real and imagined.

"Have you heard from Paul on your photo studio idea yet?" Sari said. "I'd love to bring the boys in for annual photos."

Alana didn't talk about it much, but photography was her passion. Initially, she'd dreamed of traveling the world taking photos of poverty-stricken countries and wild African animals. Her parents had quickly squashed her dream, reminding her she'd need to be with a professional journalism organization. This meant getting her degree, and Alana had always struggled in school. Plus, photojournalism was a competitive field and, according to her parents, an impractical profession which could be dangerous, too.

Instead, Alana regularly took photos of beautiful shoes, which often looked more like art than footwear. She also took photos of some of the most beautiful places in Chatelaine. She posted them on Instagram on a special account she called Life in Pictures, which had a few hundred followers. And for months, Alana had campaigned for a photo studio to be added to GreatStore like the ones at the larger department stores in the city.

With the advent of cameras on every phone, photo studios had become a relic of the past. But Alana had asked around, and there was interest among residents. After all, photo studios came with props and backdrops not easily achieved without professional equipment. Not to mention, these family photos were now iconic.

"Paul said it would be too expensive, but he'd talk to 'the powers that be.'" Alana held up air quotes. "I'm not holding my breath."

Now that she was pregnant, it would be perfect,

because she could continue to work at GreatStore, which already had a daycare center for its employees. She'd have the best of both worlds—a secure job she adored, a place for her child and work that was her passion.

"Tell Paul I'd gladly bring in the boys for photos. I miss those places. My parents used to drag us in every year for the family photo."

"I'll give him the feedback. Hey, I'm on my break and wanted to talk to you about something." She scanned the area, to confirm no one else was close enough to hear, but lowered her voice anyway. "I haven't told anyone yet, not Paul or anyone else here. But... I'm pregnant."

Sari stopped in the middle of tagging a skintight little black dress that probably left little to the imagination. Alana hadn't seen it before today, or she might have already bought it. It would have been wasted money as she couldn't possibly wear it now.

Sari let go of the dress, her brow creased in worry. "Oh, honey. Are you okay?"

"Yes." Alana straightened. "I know it won't be easy, but I'm going to do this on my own."

"And the father?" Sari quirked a brow.

"Patrick, my ex. He left town right after I told him. Pretty sure he left skid marks on the road as he sped away. I have no idea where he is, but let's just say he won't be in the picture."

"I'm sorry." Sari put a hand on each of Alana's

shoulders. "I tend to be very independent, but I remember how difficult it was in the beginning. And I know how important it is to have support. A solid team and a network in place. It takes a village and all that. You can count on *me*. What about your parents? Will they be supportive?"

"I haven't told them yet."

"No? How far along are you?"

"Thirteen weeks." Alana lowered her gaze.

She'd known for twelve long weeks she was pregnant and still hadn't told her parents. In her defense, she'd told Patrick the moment she'd learned, and looked what happened there.

Sari made a clucking but soothing sound. "You're going to start showing soon. Especially since you're so tiny in the first place."

"I've been wearing the right clothes to conceal." Today she wore an empire-waisted dress that nicely camouflaged her swelling belly. She'd told Paul a couple of weeks ago that she'd lost her purple work apron and had ordered a new one, and so far, he hadn't bugged her about it again.

"And you *have* hidden it well. I had no idea."

"I want to tell my parents, but… I hate to disappoint them again. This is not at all what they'd pictured for me."

"Listen, whatever you've imagined in your mind, it's not going to be half as bad as you think. If your parents are angry, it will only be at the situation, mostly directed to the deadbeat dad. Speaking as a mother, I know I would be furious. But don't mistake that as anger toward *you*. A family's emotional support is key but your chosen family can come in many forms. If I still had my mom and dad, believe me, I would have told them. I'd probably be living with them now, too. You should tell your parents, soon, and I promise it won't be nearly as horrible as you're thinking it will be."

Poor Sari. It must be so hard for her to be raising her boys without a family for support. At least Alana had her parents even if they no longer lived nearby.

"Okay. I know you're right. I'll call them soon."

"It's a good thing we have the employee daycare center here. I don't know how I'd manage without it. Before this, I hopped around from job to job needing flexible hours. But with the center right here, I'm not going anywhere. Hey, and our kids might grow up together!" She elbowed Alana.

The thought made her smile. Without the daycare center right at GreatStore, Alana would have to move back in with her parents. They wouldn't like it, of course, but they'd feel obligated. She could only imagine how they'd welcome *that* news. Not just one boomerang kid coming home, but two.

"Let's chat again later." Sari gave Alana a comforting hug as a coworker approached. "You have my number. Call me anytime."

With that, her break was over, and Alana went back to work to sort through sexy push-up bras. Maybe someday she'd be able to wear this kind of lingerie again.

Just not anytime soon.

## Chapter Three

Coop couldn't stop thinking about Alana. Every morning and night, at work and off work.

It had been three days since she turned him down for a second date, and he still couldn't stop reliving that kiss. He was puzzled, because her response *showed* him how she felt. But her words told him a different story. Those words had made a choice he didn't understand. She liked him, that much was clear. No woman kissed a man the way she had if she didn't feel the pull of attraction and chemistry.

He felt this magnetic tug to her and though she might not feel as intensely as he did, there was *something* there. Maybe he'd insulted her somehow. He must have done something wrong. She'd seemed to enjoy herself on the lakeside picnic, but had he been too cheap on the actual date? He could have sprung for dinner in a restaurant. He might not have received his inheritance, but he wasn't exactly destitute. He'd merely been trying to be creative and romantic with the picnic, not cheap. Had she taken it the wrong way? As if she wasn't worth spending more money on?

He had half a mind to remind her he was about to come into a big inheritance, but she did seem aware of it. The entire town knew. While that windfall seemed like a good reason for any woman to want a second date with him, he didn't want anyone who only wanted him for his future money. With Alana, her rejection had led him to believe that she wasn't at all interested in him for his wealth. And damn it, that in and of itself made her even more attractive to him.

Now, he finished mucking his favorite quarter horse's stall and led him back inside. It was the end of his workday.

"A nice clean bathroom for you, Arrow. You are welcome."

Coop usually worked from five in the morning until two in the afternoon mucking stalls, mending fences, vaccinating livestock, herding and tagging cattle, and all his usual husbandry jobs on the Rusty Spur Ranch. Every now and then he grabbed overtime hours, but not today. Today, he had plans to drop by GreatStore, where Alana worked, and find her. Everything worth having was worth working hard for, and he would try again for a second date.

When he arrived at GreatStore, he went down several aisles, scanning the departments for a beautiful blonde. No Alana anywhere. It could be her day off, of course, and maybe he was wasting his time here. He could ask one of the store employees but didn't want to look like a stalker. Still, he'd begun to feel like an idiot walking around, and people were beginning to stare.

"Can I help you?" a clerk asked.

"I'm good." He waved her away.

On his second time around the store, he picked up a bag of dog food in the pet department, because he could always use another. This way, maybe salesclerks would stop asking to help, assuming he'd found what he needed.

"Hey, Coop."

He turned at the sound of the sweet voice and there was Alana, in the ladies' lingerie section by all the sexy bras and panties. *Gulp.*

"Hey, there." He walked over to her with his bag of food and tried not to lose his focus while standing this close to women's lingerie. "How are you?"

"Oh, busy working." She waved her hand at the display with a grin. "What are you doing here?"

"I needed dog food."

"Anything else? Because we're kind of far from the pet department." She held up a lacy red bra with a smirk. "Or are you shopping for a special someone?"

He immediately pictured the silky bra barely covering Alana's perky breasts. His mouth on that soft material, pulling it back with his teeth...

"Coop?" She pulled him out of his fantasy.

He cleared his throat. "Depends. Would you model it for me?"

"Me?" She laughed.

"How else can I be sure it will fit you?"

She cocked her head, biting her lower lip. "You want to buy me lingerie?"

"Maybe. But only if I get to see you wearing it first."

She snorted. "Not going to happen, buddy."

"You sure?"

"Well. Maybe if you let me buy you a banana hammock. You'd have to model it for me, too. You know what that is, don't you?"

Dear Lord. He was afraid he did, and he'd have to be knocked unconscious to wear one of those.

She burst into laughter. "You okay, Coop? You went a little red in the face there."

Oh, well, how nice. She was *teasing* him. A tease was something he understood on a most basic level.

"You're cute, you know?"

"I'm sorry to laugh at you, but it's pretty funny how men behave around lingerie. It's perfectly harmless on the hanger."

"You mean I'm not the only one who gets tongue-tied around all the panties?"

Oh, damn. Poor choice of words. He might have blushed.

"No, you're not the only one. Most men seem to become blind while they walk by the lingerie. It's kind of like looking at the sun, I suppose. Too bright and painful to stare straight into."

"Is that so?" He set down the bag. "Well, I've been thrown off a horse a time or two, so a little lace won't scare me. These panties don't bother me at all."

*Liar. They bothered him in the sense he couldn't stop picturing Alana wearing them and this wasn't exactly the time or the place.*

"Then you have courage under silk." She smirked.

He cleared his throat. "Actually, the truth is I came here for another, probably much more important reason."

"What's that?"

"I want to ask you to go out with me again. A second date. This time you didn't win me. Maybe I can win *you*."

She lowered her gaze but smiled almost shyly. "I don't know."

"This time you can let *me* decide if you're the right kind of girl for me. Do you like to ride horses?"

"I love to ride." She looked up, her eyes brightening, but then she totally shut down. "Oh. But I… I can't."

This was plain weird. Alana had a bit of a reputation as a woman who loved fun with zero commitments—precisely what he wanted and needed right now. He was far from ready to settle down with any one woman. She was probably not ready to settle down, either. Neither one of them was dating anyone else, and for the first time they could be together. But apparently, she wasn't on board the way he was.

"Fine, I won't bother you anymore. I get it. You don't want to go out with me. But did I do something wrong on our date? Tell me."

"No, Coop. You didn't do anything wrong. I had a wonderful time."

"Then if you're not going out with me again, I'd like to know why. I want a good reason, too. Do a good deed. It'll help me in the future. I don't get this, because you're the perfect kind of girl for me."

Her eyes flashed in anger, and she put one hand on her hip. "Why am I the perfect girl for you? What have you heard?"

"Nothing." He held up his palms in a surrender gesture. "You're funny and easy to talk to. I happen to be a fan of those two characteristics. That's all. Is that all right?"

He'd obviously deeply offended her somehow,

either by the statement or something else. He might never know why.

"Oh. Sure, that's all right. It's just that I…" Her gaze flitted around the store. "Yeah, okay, I'll go out with you again."

This time, *he* wasn't so sure. Maybe he'd simply worn her down. But he didn't want to guilt her into another date. He just wanted a good reason for the rejection. This way he could be sure never to repeat whatever offensive thing he'd done.

"Are you sure about this? I don't want to pressure you into going out with me."

"Just…call me. Okay? But I should get back to work now." She held up a black thong with a wicked grin. "The panties are waiting for me."

"Smart-ass."

But he walked away with a smile.

Yikes. That hadn't gone well. Alana finished pulling out the last stack of bras from the vendor's box. She'd had her fun with Coop for a few minutes. For a moment there, she'd been her old self again. Teasing him for acting like he'd come upon a bear in the woods when he found her in the lingerie department. Only he seemed to still bring out that playful quality in her. Then she'd remembered. *You're going to be a mother, genius. Pull back on the flirty talk.* When he'd made the statement that she was the "right kind of girl" for him, she'd been thrown back to the time when greatly exaggerated rumors about her sex life were rampant.

She couldn't come up with a good enough reason why she couldn't go on a horseback ride that didn't involve confessing she was pregnant and afraid she might hurt her baby. And honestly, he'd been so sincere in wanting to know what he'd done wrong when he'd been perfect.

So, she'd agreed to a second date, even if it still wasn't a good idea.

Besides, he'd been so adorable standing there with his bag of feed. A big and muscular man among the tiny and delicate lingerie. Yet somehow, even in his hat, jeans and flannel shirt, he looked like he belonged there. She flashed back to Coop's big, callused hands and the way they'd been gentle when they held her hands. When they had danced.

He had a way of looking at her that made her feel precious, like she was made of fine china, and he worried he might accidentally break her. She'd never had a guy take such care with her and be so romantic. The picnic on the lake, dancing in front of his beaming headlights. It was like something out of a country song.

She'd go on a second date, because in her book that still meant no funny business. They'd have fun, maybe another one or two of those amazing kisses, and she'd end the night with another great memory. She was creating a metaphorical bank of those, because in a few months, she imagined, she wouldn't ever have fun again.

She'd have a baby to care for and prioritize. Looking for love would have to come last because she'd never make the mistake her parents did with her. All her focus would go to her child. Even if she wished for romance and a man who loved both her and their baby, it was too late for that now. She was having the baby without the man in her life to love them both.

Coop wasn't the father, and he also wasn't the kind to settle down and have a family. He thought she was funny, and easy to be with, but she probably wouldn't be either of those things in her last trimester. Or after the baby started waking up for midnight feedings.

"But you're worth it, little one," she whispered as she rubbed her baby bump.

When she clocked out of work and passed by Paul's office in the back, she briefly considered telling him she'd need to go on maternity leave in a few months. He was a fair boss, doing his best to take the place of the irreplaceable Lincoln Fortune Maloney. Paul deserved all the advance notice she could give him.

His door was open, so she knocked briefly. "Hey, boss? A word?"

He waved her in. "I wanted to talk to you anyway."

"Uh-oh. Everything okay?" She came in and shut the door.

Paul crossed his arms. "Where's your apron?"

The ugly purple apron employees wore had never been her favorite, but Alana had stopped wearing it last month. Tying it around her waist emphasized her growing belly.

"I told you, I had to order new ones because I lost mine."

"All *three* of them?"

"Um, well, I spilled something on the other two, and the stains won't come out."

If that sounded pathetic, Paul seemed to be giving her a pass, nodding with understanding.

"Okay, fine. But start wearing your apron the minute it arrives. It's part of the uniform."

"Sure. So…any word on the photo studio idea?"

"I brought it up at our last marketing meeting, and I haven't heard back." He shuffled some papers on his desk. "Patience, grasshopper."

*Grasshopper?*

Paul was a big fan of old movies and forever making strange references which she never understood. "Okay, thanks for trying."

"Anything else?"

*I'm pregnant, so I'm going to be taking a little time off in a few months.*

The words wedged in her throat until she felt she

might choke on them. No, she'd wait another day. One more day wouldn't make a difference. Besides, her parents should be told first. She'd do that tonight for sure.

"Nope, that's it. See you tomorrow." She smiled and went out the door.

But when Alana phoned her parents that night, neither one of them answered the phone, so she left a message.

"Um, Mom? Dad? I...hope you're doing well. I know we talked last night, but...well, you're getting old, let's face it. I have to...um, check on you. Anyway, call me!"

They were probably otherwise occupied, even if it was only late afternoon and they'd probably just gotten home from work. That never stopped those two. She used to come home from school and find their bedroom door closed, Barry White playing softly in the background. *So* humiliating.

Alana's cell pinged, and she found a text from her old friend Lucy:

I sent you an invite for the baby shower. Are you coming or not?

Another thing she'd forgotten to do. RSVP. Lucy had suddenly gone all Emily Post on everything. Alana had planned to call and had forgotten to do that, too. It wasn't like she didn't have a few other things on her mind. She quickly typed a text back.

I'll be there. What do you need? This is the second baby, so you probably already have everything.

Lucy replied quickly.

We're registered at GreatStore. Can you use your employee's discount to get me that cute little elephant-themed SpaceSaver high chair?

Alana would need one of those herself before long, but hopefully Lucy would be kind enough to throw *her* a baby shower. Or possibly let her use it secondhand. She replied, Sure.

A moment later, Lucy was video calling her. Alana picked up to the smiling face of her old friend. Lucy had changed so much since the days when they'd go out drinking and dancing to meet their future husbands. Now she wore her dark hair short and rarely put on any makeup. She claimed her husband preferred her that way.

"How do I look?" Lucy brought the camera down to her huge belly.

Oh, Lord. That's what Alana would soon look like but worse. Lucy was taller and handled any extra weight better. Still, her belly button was an outie now.

"You're glowing," Alana lied, because she hoped people would lie to her, too, when she got to this stage of her pregnancy.

"That's what Rocco says. Hey, I'm sorry about Patrick. But didn't I warn you about him?"

"Yeah, you did." Alana sighed.

"Not marriage material. That's exactly what I told you, but did you listen?"

"No."

She hadn't been looking for marriage at the time, just someone to love and who might love her in return.

One of Alana's greatest fears was that it wasn't the men she chose who weren't marriage material— it was *her*.

"I wish I'd listened to you."

"Are you finally going to let me fix you up? Rocco's friend is looking for a special someone."

*Oh, Lord, no.*

"Um, actually, I have a date."

"You mean Cooper from the bachelor auction? That doesn't count. You basically hired an escort. He is pretty cute, though, I admit. Worth every penny."

"Well, he asked me out again," Alana said defensively.

Why *couldn't* she get a guy like Cooper Fortune Maloney?

"Really?"

"Yeah, and he kissed me, too. I didn't pay for a kiss. Just a date."

"Oh, wow. Probably a pity kiss."

Alana felt her face grow hot, and she bristled at the tone in Lucy's voice. Ever since getting married, Lucy had adopted this superior outlook. Of all her friends, Lucy was the only one with an attitude about having "settled down." She even referred to their single lifestyle when Lucy and Alana were roommates as "the time I was truly lost" and "BR." Before Rocco. As if anything that happened before she met and married her husband didn't count.

"You know what, Lucy? You're…you're…you're just plain wrong! You can't be right about everything all the time. You're my oldest friend, but sometimes, I don't know, I just… You know what? Never mind!" Alana pressed the button to disconnect the video call.

She needed better friends.

Alana was on her second bowl of ice cream, watching *The Great British Baking Show* and wondering if she should bake brownies, when Lucy texted her apology.

I'm sorry. That was mean. Blame it on baby brain. I'm sure Coop kissed you because he wanted to. You're very pretty and all. But I wanted to gently remind you that just like Patrick, Coop Fortune Maloney is NOT marriage material. Love you! xo

Alana picked up her phone and shouted into it, "I know!"

But damned if she didn't like him anyway.

## Chapter Four

With most women, normally Cooper would wait a day or two, but he didn't want Alana to change her mind and call him with some excuse to cancel their date. He'd called the next day and invited her to the ranch where he worked. On his day off, he had time to relax, maybe take her for a ride if she'd changed her mind and show her all the animals who meant so much to him.

When he picked her up, she was dressed in tight jeans and a loose, blousy top, her blond hair pulled into a high ponytail. No matter what she wore, he couldn't help but think she looked like a cover model from one of those magazines his sister, Justine, used to read. Breathtaking. Alana had listened to him and worn plainer boots today, as he'd warned her life on a ranch could be a messy proposition.

Best to leave the fancy footwear at home. He vowed to prevent her from stepping in any pies but didn't want to risk her pretty new boots.

"Is this where you work?" she asked when he pulled off the road and drove down the bumpy lane to the area in the back of the barn where he normally parked.

He nodded. "The Rusty Spur is a fairly large operation. They're mostly a dairy farm but do a bit of everything. The owner has about twenty head of cattle, some horses and goats."

"I think goats are so cute."

"Yeah? What are your feelings about horses?"

"I love those, too." She bit her lower lip and wouldn't meet his eyes.

He recalled the bright shimmer in her eyes when he'd mentioned a horseback ride, then the switch straight into panic mode. Puzzling.

"Did you have a bad experience with a horse?"

"No. Why?"

He shut off the truck and turned to her. "Nothing. But if you don't feel like riding, we can do that another time."

"*Another* time?"

She seemed genuinely surprised he might want to see her again.

"Why not? If you're like me, you're going to love this place. Today, I'll just introduce you to the horses."

He waved to one of the ranch hands out working the field today. One of the many perks of the job was the owner allowed them to exercise the horses whenever they liked. Usually, Coop had too much to do on a regular workday, unless he stayed late, which he often did. Something about riding a horse always steadied him, no matter what kind of a day he'd had.

Alana walked closely beside him, and he found that he touched her every chance he had. His hand low on her back, turning to lead her toward the stables. Or his hand on her shoulder, pointing to show her the goat pen in the distance. They stopped at the corral where Billy, one of the trainers, was working with their latest quarter horse.

"Exactly what kind of work do you do around here?" Alana said, whipping out her phone and taking some photos of the horse.

Cooper braced his arms against the corral as he watched Billy work.

"Everything needed. The guys and I tackle it all. Mendin' fences, milking, mucking stalls, moving cattle."

"Herding cattle on a horse? You mean you're *literally* a cowboy?"

He chuckled. "Guess so. And I hate to dispel the fantasy, but lots of times we use the ATVs. It's just cheaper and more efficient. But I'll never turn down the chance to ride a horse."

"Do you have your own?"

He broke out in hearty laughter. "Horses and their upkeep and maintenance make them expensive. But as soon as I come into my inheritance, I'm going to buy the biggest ranch I can find in Chatelaine and a passel of horses. It's what I've always wanted."

"You didn't mention it the other night when I asked what you were going to do with all your money."

"Didn't I?" He shrugged it off. "I always wanted to be a rancher. Growing up, we never had much money, since my mother was a single mom."

"I remember. Your mother raised all you boys and Justine entirely on her own."

She sounded incredulous, as if it was something she'd just now heard, but everyone in town pretty much knew the sad Maloney story. Rick Maloney, his father, the no-account man who one day walked out and simply left his entire family. In their small town, no one forgot this kind of scandal. Most people were kind enough not to talk about it anymore.

"I know, right? But she wasn't left with much of a choice, either. Rick didn't leave anything behind for us, not that we ever had much to begin with."

"That must have been so difficult for her. For all of you."

"Yes, particularly hard for her was being mother to the most troublesome boy in the world." He hooked a thumb to his chest.

"You?" She laughed. "I don't think so."

"Believe it. I was a troublemaker from the get-go. They say I was born screaming and kicking. My mother couldn't put me down for the first three months or I'd scream to remind her I was there.

Maybe I was worried she'd forget me." He chuckled. "I had two older brothers, don't forget."

"I think that's all babies, isn't it? They need attention."

"No idea. I don't know anything about babies."

"So...your father was *never* in the picture?"

"He was, but I was only four when he left us. My younger brother, Damon, doesn't even remember our father. He took off right before my sister was born and divorced my mother. The story is one more kid was one too many for him."

Alana drew in a sharp breath. "I don't remember hearing these details. He took off when your mother was *pregnant* with Justine?"

"Yeah."

Cooper didn't know how they'd arrived on his least favorite subject on the planet. His father, Rick. He never talked about this stuff with anyone other than family. It was in the past, where he liked to store all painful memories. He preferred moving forward and not spending too much of his time and energy looking back.

"They say every kid needs a father," he told her, "but look at me. I did fine."

The one good thing his father had accomplished in his life he literally had nothing to do with. He just happened to be the illegitimate son of Wendell Fortune. Rick Maloney was probably rolling over in his grave at having missed out on receiving the inheritance. Still, it was ironic that after his death,

Rick had inadvertently, through no fault of his own, wound up leaving a fortune to his sons and daughter.

"Is it true he had to be declared dead because you never heard from him again?"

"The rumors are true. Rick sent divorce papers by courier to my mother. Classy, huh? He started a new life, away from us, but he wasn't any more successful. He took off after an argument with his second ex-wife and she never saw him again. She finally tracked him down to California and she's the one who had him declared legally dead five years ago after a motorcycle accident roughly a year before that. Apparently, he was driving along a cliff, and they found the wreckage when it washed up on the shore, but never found his body."

"I'm sorry, Coop."

Wanting to divert the focus from his father, he asked her, "Your parents are great, right?" Most everyone in town knew Mr. and Mrs. Searle, a loving couple who had walked everywhere holding hands.

"Yeah, pretty wonderful. Unless you're their daughter."

His instinct was to lower his arm from the fence and wrap it around her, because she sounded a little lost. What was so depressing about having great parents?

"Why's that?" he asked as he turned to her.

"They kind of ignored me but had such high expectations at the same time. I never could live up to them. To be fair, for a long time I didn't even try.

They made it too easy when they didn't pay much attention to me unless I was doing something wrong."

"Ah, a familiar story."

To Coop, memories of his father before he'd left them always involved him having done something wrong. Later, his mother had confided in Coop that she'd always believed he was simply trying to get his father's attention.

Alana shrugged it off. "I'm not feeling sorry for myself. I was lucky to be raised by both parents and I know it."

"Nothing's perfect, though."

"Right. But I do want to have what they had. Someday. They're still so in love. None of my friends' parents were anything like mine. Mine couldn't keep their hands off each other."

Cooper chuckled. "And that's a *problem*?"

"Try being their daughter." She shook her head. "Embarrassing."

There was something so vulnerable about her in that moment that he ached for her. While it didn't seem like such a burden to him, he tried to put himself in her place. It was nearly impossible because he'd had a mother who focused first and almost entirely on her children. He guessed there had to be balance in a healthy family. No matter how in love you were, children shouldn't be ignored. Especially not one as sensitive as Alana.

He traced the curve of her face, the silky softness of her skin a sharp contrast to his rough skin. She studied him, soft eyes and a beautiful mouth giving him a tender, sweet smile. He had to pull himself away from stealing another bone-melting kiss. Instead, he took her hand in his and tugged her along.

"C'mon. Let me introduce you to my favorite horse."

Alana nuzzled the white forelock of Coop's favorite horse, a painted pinto mare the owner had named Thunder, but whom Cooper secretly called Oreo. She took a photo, of course, because damn if she didn't resemble the cookie.

"She's an old girl but well trained because she raced in her younger days. A thoroughbred." Coop handed Oreo a salt lick. "Very gentle. She's retired now, enjoying the good life."

The past few minutes of revealing personal talk from Coop had shaken her. He'd been so open with her, and she with him. She'd never confessed both her pride and embarrassment at her parents' close and intense relationship. Never confessed that she'd wanted that for herself someday. Her parents were so wrapped up in each other that no one could splinter their world. She wanted someone, too, who wouldn't walk away when there was trouble.

Who wouldn't walk away when he learned she was pregnant with another man's child.

For the first time, she thought maybe Cooper could be that man. After having been through the experience of his own father leaving his mother, he would have a keen understanding of Alana's situation. Of course, Coop's mother, Kimberly, had been married to Rick Maloney at the time, unlike Alana. Kimberly might have logically expected her husband to stick around since they already had four children. Alana had never had such an expectation from Patrick. Just a hope and prayer that he'd do the right thing and at least help her out financially.

When Coop talked about owning a ranch, his milk chocolate–brown eyes shimmered, making him even more attractive. He wasn't only interested in week-long parties in Cancún and blowing all his money on booze and women. Coop had a plan for his future, one that still seemed to involve hard work, if he wanted to be a rancher. Deep down, she realized, he was a man of character like his brothers. Like Lincoln, the best boss she'd ever had. She shouldn't be surprised, and hope bloomed inside her for the first time in weeks.

He showed her all over the ranch, taking time to introduce each animal as though they were a special friend of his. They lingered over the goats, and he let Alana feed them, their rough-as-sandpaper tongues taking each morsel from her hand.

"This is Milo," Cooper said. "And over here is Cosmo."

"Interesting names. Yours, or the owners?"

"Mine. They don't name any of the goats."

They ran into a few of his coworkers, and Coop introduced her to everyone. Coop also showed her the barn that housed the milking pens where one of his friends was at work on a cow.

A little boy of about three or four ran inside, chased by a man. Coop introduced Alana to Otis, a fellow cowboy who often brought his son over on his day off to see the animals.

"Hey, buddy." Cooper bent to fist-bump the little boy, then rose to introduce her. "Alana, meet Mikey."

"Hi, I'm four," the little boy said, splaying four fingers in the air. "And I love cows."

He was adorable. Alana was hoping for a girl, but this little one made her think having a boy might not be so terrible. He was dressed in cute little Western boots and a hat.

"I like cows because they go, 'Moo! Moo!' When I grow up, I'm going to be a farmer." Mikey jumped up and down like he had a spring in his pants. "Daddy! Oh, Daddy! I'm four now so I can milk the cow! Yes, yes, yes!"

"No, son. I didn't say you could milk the cow when you're four. I said you had to be *older* to do that job." Otis chuckled, tousling the boy's mop of red hair.

"No, you *said*!" Mikey stomped his foot. "I'm older now. Before I was three. Now I'm four. I. Want. To. Milk. The. Cow!"

"Hoo boy," Otis said. "Somebody isn't minding his manners. Wait till Mama hears about this."

This didn't help the situation, and Mikey's face turned beet red right before he wailed so loudly that Alana jumped.

"Excuse me, y'all." Otis picked up a screaming

Mikey and carried him out of the barn, his little jeans-clad legs kicking in the air. "Someone needs a nap."

Cooper laughed and raked a hand down his face. "Oh, man. *Kids.* I'm glad I don't have any yet. Figure someday I will, probably when I'm forty. Plenty of time for all that, right?"

Alana froze and probably had the same expression Mikey did when he'd been told he couldn't milk the cow.

Utter and crushing disappointment.

"Um, sure. Yeah. Plenty of time."

*For some of us.*

Coop drove her home about lunchtime. "Want to stop by the Chatelaine Bar and Grill for some grub?"

It was the nicest restaurant in town, a place she couldn't afford, and Coop was sweet to offer.

"No, I should get home. I have to…do my laundry." She cleared her throat. "It's laundry day."

"Don't you eat lunch on laundry day?"

"Sure, something quick and on the go. Just take me home, please."

No point in torturing herself any longer. Coop continued to be too much of a temptation, and clearly, he wasn't anywhere near ready to go to the places she would soon visit. A place with screaming babies who'd proudly sound louder than Mikey did today. Frequent diaper changes. Sleepless nights. He couldn't have been any clearer today. He wasn't ready to be a father. So, forget the fact that he was gorgeous, sex on a stick and a man of good character. It wasn't fair to saddle him with a child who wasn't even his own.

Alana was going home to eat some ice cream. And pout. Maybe, like Mikey, she too needed a nap.

Coop walked her to the front door, held her hand and went in for a kiss. She should push him away. She should tell him to get lost. Lie and say that she didn't even like him. What she should do, if she could find the nerve, was tell him the whole truth about her pregnancy. He would understand and be gone before the door shut all the way. All she had to do to get rid of him was tell him her little growing secret, and his truck would probably leave skid marks on his way out of here. When he learned her situation, he'd never see her in the same way again.

But she couldn't tell him. Not now. At the very least, she had to tell her parents before she told Coop. Even if he wouldn't want to be with her afterward, she had no doubt he could be a good friend. Someone to commiserate with.

But instead of telling him to back off, she enjoyed the kiss, falling headfirst into a place of desire and deep longing. Responding equally to her passion, he pulled her close, one hand on her behind. They were hip to hip, nearly molded to each other. She kissed him so hard he nearly lost his hat. Clutching his shirt, she let every sexual frustration out until they were boiling. It got pretty heated, right there on her front porch, and she would love to invite him inside.

But that wasn't going to happen.

He was trouble, for her future and most of all her heart. She couldn't allow herself to get invested in this man even though the strength of her attraction to him stunned her.

She pulled away, a little breathless. "'Bye."

He looked a bit stunned, poor guy, scratching his jawline like he was trying to figure out a complicated algebra word problem.

"I can't come inside?"

"I'm sorry. Not today because…well, I… Remember the laundry."

"Laundry, huh." He looked at her through narrowed eyes.

Big shock, he didn't believe her. She was such a bad liar. All her parents ever had to do was ask, "Is that what *really* happened, Alana?" and she'd fold like, well, clean laundry.

It was only date number two, anyway, despite her temptation to break every rule for Coop.

*Date number three before any hanky-panky, fella.*

"Thank you again for a great day."

He tipped his hat. "You're welcome, Alana. You have fun with the laundry."

"Thanks."

She cringed, then turned, hand on the doorknob and heard his voice behind her, low and smooth.

"You're a bad liar, you know?"

She groaned and pressed her forehead to the door, then turned to him. "I know."

"But I like that." He pointed to her as he walked backward to his truck. "I'll call you."

## Chapter Five

Coop decided that the brush-off today was more than enough reason to drop by the Chatelaine Bar and Grill for a cold beer. Alone. He'd lick his wounds and wonder why fake laundry was more important than inviting him inside for more kissing and whatever else might develop. Clearly, she'd lied, but he still couldn't figure out why. She was attracted to him, because those kisses and passionate groping on her end couldn't be faked. No matter how good a liar she might be.

When Coop arrived, he found his younger brother, Damon, behind the bar pulling a day shift. Normally he worked nights. Besides Justine, the youngest, Coop and Damon were the only two who had yet to receive their inheritance. A bartender by trade, his brother had zero trouble with the ladies. Kind of like Coop before Alana. He might assume he'd lost his game, but then he'd flash back to Alana's fists clutching his shirt as she kissed him, practically ripping off a button.

The few times he'd been in the bar and grill, Coop had decided he liked this place, and he felt as comfortable here as on the ranch. The interior was dark with warm colors, wood walls and a bar made from one long and perfect piece of oak. The montage of photos on the wall from the town's silver mines meant something to him now. Before, they were simply photos of the town's history. Someone else's life. Now they were a part of his own heritage, and the idea never failed to amaze him.

"Hey, bro." Damon set a napkin down. "What'll you have?"

"Just a beer."

"Care to be more specific? We have fifty types. IPA? Domestic? Imported?"

"Make it cold. Surprise me."

"Easy to please, that's what I like." Damon reached behind him for a bottle of Corona, uncapped and set it down in front of Coop. "Want to tell me who spit in your Cheerios this morning?"

"It shows?"

"You don't look like your usual happy self." Damon crossed his arms. "C'mon, now. Tell Damon all about it. It's my job to listen."

Coop snorted. "I thought your job was head bartender."

"I double as the neighborhood therapist for everyone here. Everybody knows that. Lay it on me, brother."

"No big deal. It's a girl, of course. What clsc?"

"*You?* Girl trouble?"

"Not usually. First time for everything, I guess." Coop fiddled with the napkin, pushing it around in a circle with this thumb.

"Interesting. Who's the lucky lady?"

"Alana. I don't know, maybe she's playing hard to get." He took off his hat and ran a hand through his hair, then plopped it back on. "I mean, is that even a thing anymore?"

"A girl playing hard to get?" Damon leaned toward the bar, splaying his arms out. "Maybe. Some girls play games. It's what makes them so much fun. But Alana? We're talking about Alana Searle, right?"

"Yep."

"Dude, what do you mean? You two seemed pretty cozy the night of the auction. At least you weren't won by one of the Silver Ladies like I was." He hooked a thumb to his chest. "Humiliating."

The Silver Ladies were a sweet group of elderly women who were regulars at the Chatelaine Bar and Grill. They had a walking club, and according to Damon, ordered one glass of wine and a salad.

Then they'd go home to watch their TV shows. They were perfectly harmless, though, and Damon was overreacting.

"What are you complaining about? You had the highest bid of the evening."

"From an eighty-two-year-old widow who wanted to impress her friends with a younger man. She's calling herself a cougar and says it's all thanks to me."

"Laura Lee is a sweet woman." Coop bit back a laugh.

"She could be my grandmother." Damon crossed his arms. "All night long she talked about her grandchildren."

"Back to me. I have a problem, and you were going to be my therapist."

"Oh, yeah. Alana. Damn, I wish *she* would have won me." He gazed off into the distance, a little smirk on his face, and Coop wanted to wipe that smug fantasy right out of his head.

He focused instead on his situation. "I don't know what I'm doin' wrong. I've been a perfect gentleman, but it's been two dates now and she won't even let me through the front door."

"Well, from what I know about Alana, she isn't particularly hard to get." Damon gave the bar a wipe. "She's kind of like…you. Pretty much your female equivalent. Looking for a good time."

It was what Coop had also heard through the

grapevine. If one wanted to listen to the rumors, she had a reputation for dating rivaling his own. Secretly, he'd hoped to see a little of that action, if he were being honest. They were two consenting adults, free of any other relationships. She was gorgeous and available. He was…not gorgeous, but available.

"You should know, she doesn't deserve that reputation."

"Damn. I'm sorry, man." Damon slowly shook his head.

"Tell me about it."

Cooper would have to try harder. Step it up. She was worth it. He really liked this girl, more than he could ever recall liking anyone else in his entire life.

Maybe what Alana needed was proof he wasn't just going to sleep with her and lose her number.

Two days later, Coop called Alana and asked her out again. A *third* date. Alana wondered if he already knew her rules.

Maybe he really liked her and wasn't just fooling around with her feelings. With guys, it was hard to tell sometimes. They were always sweet to her in the beginning. Like Patrick. Yet Coop was different. Sometimes she'd swear he saw inside her with those dark laser-beam eyes, which made her paranoid he'd guess her situation before she actually told him.

Today, he'd picked her up and surprised her by announcing he was taking her to the rodeo on the grounds just outside Chatelaine. The rodeo was practically an all-day event, and she was flattered he wanted to spend that much time with her.

"When's the last time you went to the rodeo?" Coop asked as he led her to some empty seats in the stands.

"I can't even remember. My parents used to make it a yearly family event, but once I complained about going, they never made me go again."

This wasn't exactly true. There was a distinct reason they'd never brought her along again. She'd liked the rodeo fine, just not being dragged there to sit with her parents while they held hands and made googly eyes at each other like a couple of teenagers. Once, when she'd been sixteen, Alana had offered to get everyone sodas at the tent selling them. Then she accidentally-on-purpose got lost on the way. Two hours later, a very hot-looking cowboy escorted her back to her parents. *Without* drinks. Her dismayed parents had grounded her for a week that time, and Mom had delivered a stern lecture on safety.

It had been the best two hours she'd ever spent lost. The cowboy was, as she recalled, a good kisser. But nothing compared to Coop.

"You haven't been back? Don't like the rodeo?" Coop's questions chased away the memory.

"Are you kidding? What's not to like about studly cowboys roping cattle and being thrown from bulls?"

Coop chuckled. "The point is not to get thrown from the bull. It hurts like the dickens. And let me tell you, you best run if you fall off. Fast."

She shouldn't be too surprised. "You tried the rodeo?"

"It was a short career. Riding the rodeo was made for guys like me who love the spike of an adrenaline rush. But competing is expensive, and my family couldn't afford it. You can make a lot of money eventually if you're good, but it's a long shot." Coop stood. "What would you like to drink? Another soda?"

"Yes, thank you."

"Be right back."

Female eyes were on Coop the moment he walked out into the aisle, with women turning in their seats and flashing smiles and licking lips as he walked by. A young woman nearly bumped into him, and he graciously steadied her. She not-so-discreetly checked out his ass as she went on her way.

Alana chuckled, because she appreciated his behind, too, in those tight jeans. After today, she might be able to see what was under those jeans, but she couldn't do it without telling him the truth. And now that she'd waited to tell him, would he feel betrayed she'd kept her pregnancy from him?

Shannon caught Alana's eye, waved and walked

up to meet her. Dressed in skintight jeans and a top that hugged her waist and emphasized its small size, Coop's ex-girlfriend held the neck of a beer bottle as she walked, swinging her hips. Around Coop's age, she'd already been married and divorced.

"Hey, no hard feelings, okay?" Shannon said. "You won him fair and square."

"Um, thanks."

"I had a moment of amnesia that night," Shannon continued with a sigh. "Call it nostalgia, but suddenly I wanted to be with him again. For old times' sake. We were good together, but it's better that I didn't win. A waste of time, I'm sure you know. Coop isn't the kind of cowboy to ever settle down."

"Yeah, I heard."

Disappointment hit her like a weight.

It wasn't as if Lucy hadn't already reminded her. In case Alana had any doubts, here was an ex-girlfriend's warning. Everybody seemed to have Coop dialed. But they'd thought they knew her, too, and they were wrong.

"So, like, if you think you're going to nab him now because he's coming into some money, I'd think twice."

A hot spike of anger flashed through Alana. "I didn't think it once, let alone twice."

Shannon held up her palms. "All right, all right. I'm just a little protective of my ex. He's very special."

"You don't have to worry about me," Alana spit out. "We're just friends."

Was this what *everyone* thought? Did they honestly think she was low enough to go out with a man because he would be coming into money soon? So, she'd gone from her reputation as simply being the town's wild child to that of a gold digger. Awesome. The thought stung. She'd prided herself on making it on her own for years, especially after Lucy moved out. Cutting corners, doing without, saving her money. She was independent and resented anyone thinking otherwise.

"Hey, Shannon." Coop's stilted voice came from behind the other woman as he waited behind her to get to their seats.

"Oh, hey, sweetheart!" Shannon flattened her free hand against Coop's chest. "We were just talkin' about you."

"Uh-huh."

*Sweetheart?* Alana wasn't one to be jealous or possessive, but now her gut burned with something similar. Shannon moved, making room for Coop to brush by, carrying the drinks.

"See y'all!" Shannon waved as she walked away.

Alana reached for her drink, and Coop took a seat.

"Everything okay?" he asked.

She nodded. "Just your fan club. She wanted to

make sure I know there are no hard feelings since she lost the auction."

"Ignore her. And ignore everything she said about me. Shannon doesn't know me. She just thinks she does."

While Alana wondered what that meant, the rodeo began. Alana rather enjoyed the pageantry of the regal horses, their riders performing opening routines. Shortly after, the qualifying events began. Tie-down roping, bareback riding, steer wrestling, saddle bronc riding, bull riding, team roping and barrel racing. Coop happened to know who was favored to win, who was new and who had recently recovered from an injury.

Afterward, they walked around enjoying some of the vendor displays. He bought her tacos and caramel corn, and they walked hand in hand around the booths. She paused at a handmade jewelry booth, admiring a turquoise bracelet, and when they got into his truck to drive home, he surprised her with it.

He took it out of the box, draped and clasped it around her wrist. Then he took the same hand and kissed her palm. "I saw you admiring it. It's beautiful, just like you."

"You didn't have to do that. Don't spend your hard-earned money on me."

"My pleasure. I wanted you to have it."

She gazed into his warm, dark eyes, and her resistance to his charms lowered another notch. Possibly two.

"Well, thank you."

He drove her home, holding her hand the entire time.

They'd had another great date, and now here they were at her front porch again. Same place, different day. This was the arbitrary third-date rule, but nothing said she *had* to have sex tonight just because she asked him inside. She probably wouldn't, not without telling him the truth. And she still hadn't told her parents, so she had to wait a little while before telling anyone else.

Now, she reached for and held his large, callused hand in hers. The chemistry between them sparked as it did every time.

It was almost too big to fight even if she should.

He stood close, so close, until they were almost sharing a breath. Belly to belly, her fingers brushed against his jaw and the beard stubble there. He smiled, a slow and wicked grin.

She prayed he wouldn't notice her trembling hand when she put the key in the doorknob.

"Do you want to come in?"

"Yes."

He ambled inside, his big presence dwarfing the place. She saw her cottage through his eyes: tiny and cramped, filled with trinkets and secondhand furniture she hoped to replace. Someday.

"Nothing fancy, but I keep it clean."

He snorted. "You should see my place."

"But soon you'll be able to live wherever you'd like. On the ranch you want."

While she might have to move to California and live with her parents for a while. At least until she got settled and used to being a single mother. After that she'd probably always have to live close to the two people who would be her primary emotional support. But at least she had another option, and her parents, after they got over the shock, might be okay. Probably.

"Let me get you something to drink."

Shakier than she could ever recall being in her life, she grabbed a plastic tumbler from her mismatched set and filled it with cold water from the pitcher in the fridge. Coop was right behind her when she turned. He accepted the glass with a slow grin and swallowed the water in three large gulps.

"You're thirsty," she said inanely, watching the muscles work in his powerful neck.

It was better than giving voice to her hotter thoughts. Coop even had a sexy way of drinking *water*.

"And you're skittish." He set the glass down on the counter. "Don't be. I like you a lot. And I'm not going to sleep with you and stop calling. I'm not sure what the guys you dated before me were like, but I'm not like them."

"I know you're not. I'm not nervous or scared, but I don't know what gave you the idea I'm going to sleep with you because you bought me a bracelet."

He blinked, then scratched the side of his jaw. "No, I don't think that at all. Maybe I'm a little too hopeful. It's my nature. But I don't *expect* anything."

"Okay." She took his hand and led him back into the living room, sitting on her couch. "I really like you, too, by the way."

"Good." He sat beside her, his big hand settling on her knee.

She turned to him. "We can do some kissing, though. That's okay with me."

He kissed her again in his sweet and sexy way, his tongue playing with hers gently. Whenever he kissed her, she felt a powerful wave of emotion tugging her deep under. Before long the heat intensified as it always seemed to do between them, even when they were standing on the porch. The blaze grew and flickered between them, and she ripped off his hat, sinking her fingers into his thick, soft hair. She pulled him close, climbing on his lap.

Coop's hand dived under her shirt, touching bare skin, his fingers perilously close to her swelling abdomen. This slammed her back into reality, and she pulled back, panting.

"Wait."

"What's wrong? Am I going too fast? I'll slow

down—I just got caught up in the moment." He raked a hand through his hair. "I'm sorry."

"No, it's not that."

She *had* to tell him. It was time. She hadn't been fair to someone so kind and generous. Even if this was the last time she'd see him, it was wrong to hold back any longer and unfair to lead him on.

If she expected fairness and honesty from others, she had to give it first.

"There's something I have to tell you, and I'm sorry I didn't say anything before. It's just...hard to talk about."

Coop frowned, his brow furrowed. "What is it? It sounds serious."

"It is serious. Yes." She climbed off his lap and pulled her legs up to her chest. "I'm...pregnant."

Dead silence. The room was so quiet she could hear the ticking of the battered old rooster-shaped kitchen clock her grandmother had given her.

Coop looked at her once, then simply stared off into space.

"You can go now," she told him. "It's okay. I totally understand. I just wanted to tell you the truth, because you deserve to know. You've been so patient, so kind. And it isn't that I don't want to be with you, because I do. But please understand that I have to think about my baby first."

He still wasn't saying anything, so she kept talking.

"So, that's my anchor. Remember I talked about

having to grow up and when it helps to have an anchor? My baby is my anchor. I can't fool around and
be carefree anymore. Someone else is depending
on me, and it's time for me to grow up. But having
a child is a huge, life-changing thing. You have a
right to wait until you're forty." Wasn't that what
he'd said? That he'd consider having a kid when he
was forty?

"Who's…who's the father?" He still wouldn't
look at her, but at least he was talking.

"My ex-boyfriend. Patrick. The minute I told
him, he took off. I have no idea where he is."

Coop finally turned and met her eyes, his jaw
rigid. "What an ass."

Of course, he would be angry. Patrick was a reminder of what Coop's own father had done.

"Yeah, I know. But that's not your problem. *None*
of this is your problem. I just wanted you to know,
because I haven't been completely honest with you
and you've been so nice to me. I'm not really used
to that. Guys think of me as a good time and nothing else. They fool around with me and fall in love
with other women."

"That can't be true."

"Yes, it is. All my friends are married. And I
know I'm not super smart or anything, which is
maybe my own fault. My parents wanted me to get
a degree, but I've always loved working right here
in town at GreatStore. We're all like a little fam-

ily there and that was especially important to me when my parents moved. It's always been enough for me, but I'm going to do better for my baby. Because I want to be the kind of mother she or he can be proud of."

A sob formed in her throat, and Alana couldn't catch it. Not this time. She burst into tears, not in private, as usual, but in front of a *guy*. This hadn't happened since she was twelve years old and the boy she'd liked told her she was pretty but also kind of stupid.

"Oh, hey, hey. Alana. Don't do that, okay? Please don't cry, sweetheart."

She hid her face in the crook of her elbow but couldn't hold back the well of tears. She hadn't cried since she found out she was pregnant—she'd been too stunned. Apparently, the shock had worn off, and bad luck for Cooper that he had to be here when it did.

She waved him away and spoke between hiccuping sobs. "G-go. You c-can go."

"No. I'm not going anywhere."

Before Alana realized what was happening, Coop pulled her back onto his lap. His hand slid up and down her back in smooth, slow strokes. She didn't know what to do or how to act. She'd never received this kind of comforting touch from a man. But because she couldn't stop the tears, she simply sat on his lap, her face buried in the crook of his warm neck, and sobbed her heart out. She cried for her old life, cried for her unborn baby who wouldn't have a father and cried for all the mistakes she'd ever made.

Coop held her and didn't even try talking. Eventually, she pulled away and grabbed a nearby box of tissues.

"I bet this isn't what you had in mind for our third date."

He smiled, a little sadly, with those sweet puppy-dog eyes. "Not really."

"I'm sorry." She dabbed at her eyes.

"Nothing to be sorry about." Coop rose and went into the kitchen. He came back with a glass of water like the one she'd given him earlier.

She sipped, then set it down on the end table. "Thank you."

"Look, Alana. Not many people know this, but my mother was pregnant with Linc before she and my dad got married. Not the best example, because she was traditional and insisted they get married. Well, we all know how that worked out. Rick Maloney may not have run out on her the first time, but eventually, he did."

"I w-wouldn't marry P-Patrick now if he c came crawling back."

"That's smart. Guys like that don't change who they are just because they try to stick around." Coop plopped back down on the couch beside her. "Believe me."

"I know, but the thought of doing this all alone is hard, too. I see why your mother didn't want that, either."

"Sometimes it works out. I don't think she'd mind if I told you, but my sister, Justine, was also pregnant before she got married. She and Stefan are happily married now."

Alana didn't quite know what to say to that. Except accidental pregnancies worked out differently for some women. Maybe for the kind of woman men fell in love with.

"They fell in love," Alana said.

"Yeah, and it's great."

"Guys never fall in love with me."

"Well, you only need one man to fall in love with you. Once. Maybe it just hasn't happened to you yet."

"I guess that's true."

"C'mere." Coop held his arms open for her.

She folded back into his arms, accepting the warmth of his body, the solid feel of his chest as she laid her head against it. Another thing guys never did with her: cuddling.

The main reason for the carefree and wild attitude she'd adopted was that she didn't like to feel sorry for herself. Everything seemed better when she didn't let anyone see how much it hurt to feel inferior. She never had good grades and struggled in school without any help. Her parents had only wanted her to try harder, but even when she did, nothing worked. Eventually she believed that she just wasn't smart, accepting what others believed about her and making it her truth. After a while she stopped trying and played to her strengths.

No one ever hesitated to invite her to a party when they wanted to have a good time.

She excelled at fun. Well, she used to.

Poor Coop definitely hadn't gotten the fun he'd hoped for tonight.

## Chapter Six

Tonight, Coop felt absolutely slain. Alana's heaving sobs were like a wrecking ball, hitting everything in its path. It didn't help that he'd never known quite what to do when a woman cried. Tears from his sister, Justine, he could handle. He used to know how to cheer her up by reading her books in funny voices and being a reluctant participant in her lavish "tea parties." Lincoln and Max teased him endlessly for sitting on a tiny chair way too small for him. Still, it always made Justine smile to have Coop attend her tea party. But Alana wasn't *ten*.

Even though he'd rarely seen his mother cry, he could handle that, too. A hug would usually be enough. Old girlfriends had only cried in front of him when they wanted something—more time together, or a firm commitment. He saw it as manipulation and had zero sympathy for phony tears.

But Alana's tears were real and her pain raw and genuine. She inspired a deep tenderness in him. All he could think to do was hold her while she cried, his heart feeling like an apple someone had cored, sliced and diced. Eventually, her sobs subsided. They talked for a while, and afterward he simply held her against his chest, listening to the even sounds of her breathing.

"Are you hungry?" he asked, relief flooding him when the crying stopped.

"I'm more tired than hungry."

Her eyelids were half-mast. He imagined the kind of crying she'd done took a lot out of a person. She looked the way he felt after a twelve-hour day of mending fences.

"The last thing you ate was caramel corn at the rodeo." He stood. "We can do better than that. You should have something to eat. Something healthy."

In the kitchen, he banged around the cupboards until he found her pots and pans.

"What are you doing in there?" Alana called out softly.

"Making you some soup. Just sit back and let me wait on you."

This was something he could do to be useful. He found a can of soup in her cupboard. Chicken noodle soup, if even from a can, cured all manner of ills. His mother said so.

He heated then brought the soup to Alana, who hadn't moved from the couch.

"Eat."

"What about you?"

"I'll eat when I get home." He didn't want to confess he'd lost his appetite, which said something.

Jeez, she was *pregnant*. She had a *baby* growing in her belly. He was still wrapping his mind around the idea. The initial shock had passed, but now he had questions. What would she do without any family support? Where would she live? Who would take care of her? But he didn't press for answers, because if she was anything like him, she'd still be figuring this out.

To think he'd been angling to get her in bed this whole time when she had so much on her plate. No wonder she'd pushed him away, no matter how much she liked him. And the anchor analogy also made a lot more sense now. This baby would ground her. Change her. And deep down he knew, just knew, that Alana would rise to the challenge. She was going to be a good mother.

But no matter how much he liked her, he was in no way ready to be a father, and nothing could change that fact.

The honorable part of him understood he had to be fair to Alana. He couldn't string her along. He couldn't promise her something he wasn't ready to give. And he sure shouldn't stand in the way of her finding someone else. Maybe someone who was ready to be a father. Coop would swallow his attraction to her and be the friend she needed.

He might want to punch Patrick's lights out, but truthfully, he worried he might have pulled the same disappearing act at one time. Thankfully, he never had, because he'd been raised better than to shirk his responsibilities to a woman. Justine, and what she'd been through, showed him a man should own up to his duties. And the last person Coop wanted to be anything like was his father.

To be fair, though, Coop knew a new baby hadn't driven his father away. He knew why his father had left them, and he still felt responsible for it to this day. It was his own secret shame, one he'd carried around for decades.

Alana wasn't carrying his child, however, and Coop was a bit stunned that he was still here. He should hug and wish her well, then go home. But he couldn't leave her. Not like this. Some force kept him rooted here, next to her. She'd unraveled tonight.

As the middle child of the family, Coop was the peacemaker, and this was what he did. His wheelhouse. He fixed stuff. As someone who had frequently damaged said *stuff*, he'd learned how to fix everything he could.

He couldn't stop thinking of Alana's predicament and what she would do next. She still had a few months to go, he figured, and time to make a plan. Meanwhile, he wanted to be there for her. He wasn't sure why, just that he did. This sense of protectiveness for her was unexpected but he would not be one of those people in her life who'd abandoned Alana. She was sweet and kind and needed a friend. Plus, when she kissed him…colors changed.

"Why does this taste so good?" Alana asked after a spoonful or two. "I've had this soup before, and it never tasted like this. Did you add something?"

"Nope. My theory is that everything tastes better when someone else makes it for you."

"You may be right." She kept eating.

"So…um, does everyone else know you're pregnant?"

She didn't answer but just looked at him carefully, probably because he'd overstepped.

He held up a hand, palm out. "I'm sorry. It's none of my business."

She shook her head. "It's okay. I told Patrick, and since his reaction, I haven't been too excited to tell anyone else. But I did tell Sari. Since Remi quit GreatStore, and I haven't seen much of her, Sari is my only friend at work."

"She's a single mom. I bet she has a lot of great advice for you."

Alana nodded. "She suggested I tell my parents right away."

"You haven't told your *parents*?" If he sounded flabbergasted, well, he was.

Then he remembered his mother's reaction to Justine's accidental pregnancy and didn't have to wonder why Alana would be hesitant.

Justine had been hurt by their mother's lack of support when she'd confessed her pregnancy and that she'd go ahead and have the baby and raise him on her own. Coop understood why his mother was traditional and hadn't approved of Justine being a single mother, but her lack of understanding had never been okay with him.

Coop and his brothers had given Justine the emotional support she needed more than anything else, and maybe he could do more of the same here for Alana.

"It's just… I've been trying to find the right time to tell them. I promise that I will very soon."

"If you want me to help, I will."

She smiled for the first time in hours, and suddenly his chest felt like a bird was flopping around in there.

"How can *you* help?"

"I don't know. Maybe I could, um, help you come up with a script?"

"A script?" She squinted at him.

"I'm guessing you want to say this exactly the right way. To create the least amount of conflict."

"It's like you know my parents."

"Not that well, no. But…let's just say I have a little bit of experience in knowing how parents react to an unplanned pregnancy."

"Justine?"

"My mother didn't take the news well, but hey." Cooper rubbed Alana's back. "She came around. One thing you can say about grandparents is they're crazy about those grandkids. No matter when or how they arrive. You should see my mother now. She tries to get up to Rambling Rose as often as she can to see little Morgan. The kid can do no wrong. I swear she's going to spoil him."

"I hope my parents will be like that."

"Sure they will. Even when parents weren't great, they seem to get mellow with the grandkids." Cooper took her empty bowl. "I'll just put this in the kitchen for you, then I'll be going."

"Okay," Alana said around a yawn. "Thank you, Coop. You're one of the nicest guys I ever met. I definitely won the best Fortune Maloney brother."

That made him smile, because he'd only ever been called the best at getting into trouble. When it came to that, he excelled.

Coop placed the bowl in the kitchen sink, but since he was already here, he figured he could unload and reload Alana's dishwasher. It took him a while to find the places where she kept her dishes, flatware and glasses. He wiped the countertop, too.

When he strode back in the living room, Alana was curled up on the couch. Sound asleep.

For crying out loud, she even looked beautiful asleep. Like an angel. *Yes. Angel. Keep up that line of thinking.* These were the thoughts he needed whenever they ran to less pure ones. He looked around for a blanket to cover her with, but there wasn't one. Instead, he figured he'd get her to bed and under the covers.

"Alana."

She didn't budge.

"Hey, um, sweetheart. Wake up. Let's get you to bed." He nudged her, and she moaned.

He picked her up in his arms, and damn, she was a sweet little thing. For someone who helped pull cows out of mud, this was a bit like carrying air.

"Coop?" she mumbled, half asleep. "What's happening?"

"Go back to sleep. I'm just taking you to your bedroom." The door was ajar, so he shoved it open the rest of the way with his shoulder.

The postage stamp–size room fit with the rest of the house. Small but clean and neat. There were frilly blue curtains on the window facing the street and a weathered matching quilt on the bed. Everything about the room said someone on a budget lived here but tried their best to make it look homey. He remembered she'd first lived in this house with her friend Lucy, whom Coop had dated years ago for about a nanosecond. Unfortunately, he hadn't liked Lucy, whom he'd found pretty stuck-up.

Lucy had eventually moved out to get married to Rocco, leaving Alana to take care of the rent by herself. It was no wonder that every can and box of food in her cupboard was the budget store brand from GreatStore.

Coop pulled back the covers and laid Alana on the bed. She rolled over on her side and away from him, right back to snoozing. He turned to leave and noticed a stack of reading material on her nightstand. All baby books—*What to Expect When You're Expecting* and others. He opened to the bookmarked page. The second trimester. He flipped through it until he got to some images of the fetus growing inside the ever-expanding uterus. That was enough information for him. Yikes.

Under the baby books lay a tattered, dog-eared copy of a photography magazine and a fashion one. He almost laughed out loud.

*Her old life.*

But on the way home, the humor stopped.

He couldn't stop thinking about Alana, all alone, facing one of life's greatest challenges.

Despite the attraction that pulled him to her, he vowed after tonight he'd simply be the friend she needed. They couldn't have the relationship he'd pictured in the beginning, but she wouldn't have to face any of this alone.

\* \* \*

Alana woke the next morning feeling refreshed and renewed. Last night had been a cathartic event of sorts, because she hadn't cried in months. Even when Patrick walked out on her, saying, "What do you want me to do about it? How do I even know for sure it's *my* baby?" she hadn't shed a tear. Just raged at his attitude and accusation. She hadn't made this baby on her own. Two of them were responsible for her condition, thank you very much, but only one of them seemed to care.

But last night with Coop, she'd let go and enjoyed a watershed moment. Maybe it was the relief at finally telling someone else, or the sharp memory of exclusion that hit her. Too many people would think they were right about her all along—loose Alana finally got pregnant, because when you fool around that much…well, what do you expect?

No one would believe she'd only been with Patrick once. One time and that's all it took.

Coop had handled her tears better than she could have expected. Yes, he probably didn't like it, because no guy ever did. They didn't know how to fix things when a woman cried, and when a guy couldn't fix it, he didn't know what to do. But Coop hadn't run out of the house. He'd tried to help and actually found a way.

Coop was the kind of guy she'd assumed was purely on the make. Ironic, because she'd judged him the way others judged her. Lesson learned. He'd proved to be a lot more than she'd ever imagined. Coop Fortune Maloney was a little like opening a box from a discount store and finding a precious diamond inside. Completely unexpected. Utterly surprising.

It was also like finding a diamond in a discount store box and being forced to do the right thing and give it back.

It was too much to hope he'd change his mind about settling down. He was probably still interested in casual and now realized Alana couldn't sign up for that. He would be too kind to lead her on. She'd likely never hear from him again. They'd run into each other occasionally and smile and wave.

The thoughts of everything that might have been between them if circumstances were different made her heart twist painfully.

Because it was her day off, Alana straightened up and cleaned her house. It didn't take long, and as had become her habit, afterward she went to her neighbor Mrs. Garcia and knocked on her door. The elderly woman was a widow on a fixed income and couldn't afford a housekeeper. Her terrible eyesight turned out to be both a problem and a blessing in disguise, because Alana helped the woman by cleaning, and though she never asked for anything in return, from time to time Mrs. Garcia gave Alana spare canned food from the senior citizen place that gave her assistance. Alana was still too proud to apply for help, even if she would have to rethink that soon. A single mother couldn't afford pride.

"Hi, Mrs. Garcia." She strode inside with her cleaning supplies.

"Hello, honey. Would you mind starting with the vacuuming today? Last week Luigi got outside, and heaven knows what he brought in with him. I've been sneezing for a week."

Luigi was Mrs. Garcia's twenty-year-old tabby cat. It was amazing he could still walk, much less sneak outside.

Alana vacuumed, moving furniture. Then she considered she would soon have to stop lifting heavy things. She wouldn't want to hurt her baby. At least the morning sickness had finally subsided, and she no longer had to run to the bathroom every few minutes. Even though Mrs. Garcia might not notice until Alana was nine months pregnant due to her poor eyesight, the confession to Coop had her on a roll. After mopping the kitchen floor, Alana found Mrs. Garcia on the couch watching reruns of *Dr. Phil.*

She pointed to the screen. "Listen to this man, Alana. I wouldn't trust any other doctor with my medical care."

Alana froze. Dr. Phil wasn't a medical doctor and he'd let his license for psychology lapse. He was a TV doctor.

"Don't you still go to the clinic for your regular checkups?"

"Oh, yes. But for anything else, I would only trust Dr. Phil."

Alana cleared her throat. "Mrs. Garcia, I—I have something to say, and I don't want you to get upset."

"It's all right, dear. My son has already informed me Dr. Phil is famous and doesn't have time for me. As if I don't realize that. Arnie Jr. thinks I've lost my marbles as well as my eyesight."

"No…see… Mrs. Garcia? I wanted you to know I'm pregnant. So, in a few months I might not be able to come over and clean once a week."

"How lovely, dear. Children are such a blessing. And is your husband, Rocco, happy?"

Oh, dear. Occasionally Mrs. Garcia still mixed Alana up with Lucy. It was the eyesight thing, even if Lucy had never come over to help clean.

"I'm Alana," she said, deciding she'd tell Mrs. Garcia later that *she* wasn't married.

She clapped her hands and laughed. "Oh, you two girls, like twins—you're so much alike! It's enough to confuse an old lady."

After she finished cleaning, Alana let Mrs. Garcia talk her into watching another episode of *Dr. Phil*, this one in which a lottery winner had completely blown through his windfall and was now destitute.

"Imagine that." Mrs. Garcia clucked in disapproval. "Mr. Garcia worked for the post office all his life, and he made sure the house was paid for so at least I wouldn't have to worry about that after he died. I don't understand these people. How do you go through twenty million dollars? What do you spend it on?"

Alana thought of the Fortune Maloneys and their inheritance. A bit like winning the lottery. She was happy for Coop, and even if he decided to throw a party and go through all his money in a short while, he had a right. He had no obligations or commitments. She'd bet he would still be happy after all the money was gone, too.

"I think some people get talked into bad investments, just like that poor man."

She sincerely hoped no one would fleece Coop out of his inheritance, but it was something she should perhaps warn him about.

When Alana went home, she decided this was a perfect time to phone her parents and tell them about the baby. Or maybe an email would do, just a short one to pave the way. They only had to be half as supportive as Mrs. Garcia, and Alana would be fine. They'd come around to the idea.

She picked up her cell to find a text from Coop.

Are you free this weekend? I'm going to Linc's new place and Remi will be there.

She nearly dropped her phone. Coop wanted to see her again?

Hope spiked through her, but then she remembered telling him she hadn't seen much of Remi. Her friend had been so busy with Lincoln and her new life that Alana hadn't bothered her with the baby news. And Remi, a good and kind friend, would no doubt be worried.

Coop was probably trying to help Alana get additional support from her friends. Another good-guy move.

At this point, she couldn't afford to be picky, even if she'd like to be far more than his friend.

She needed all the friends she could get.

## Chapter Seven

"It's good to see you!" Remi wrapped her arms around Alana.

Alana beamed, happily accepting a hug from her old coworker and friend. Cooper had a feeling this get-together was a good idea.

They were led through the foyer of Linc's new house. Unlike what Cooper planned once he received his inheritance, Linc had purchased far more house than land. It was still modest, however, just like his brother who would never dream of showing off his newfound wealth. The ranch-style place was spread over an acre, housing a two-car garage and four bedrooms.

"You have to see this," Linc said.

They left the women in the living room while

he led Coop through the spacious kitchen and then outside to the unattached garage. Linc hit a button, and the automatic door rolled up. "Feast your eyes on this."

A couple of stadium-style recliners sat before a big-screen TV. Two large speakers sat on either side of it.

"Wow, Linc. You have a man cave."

"You got that right. Always wanted one of these. For all those games we're going to watch on the big screen. You, me, Max and Damon."

"All right. I'll bring the beer." Coop settled into one of the chairs. "So, this is what living large looks like?"

Linc plopped in the seat beside Coop. "You know me. I don't need much. Buying the Ferrari was a knee-jerk reaction to having money and you know how I love cars. But the new truck is more my style. Don't worry, your time is coming soon. Any day now."

Cooper wasn't going to lie. Sharp doubt thrummed through him, because no matter how many times he heard the promise, it was still difficult to believe someday soon he'd have his own windfall.

"Yeah, that's what Max said, too. Still, sometimes it's hard to wait."

"What are you going to do with your money? Have a huge party in Vegas?"

It was what everyone expected from him, and

Coop didn't like letting people down. "Yeah, you know me."

"Well, you're going to have a lot more money than you'll ever need but don't forget that you could also burn through the money fast if you're not careful. Start thinking of wiser ways to spend your money. I can put you in touch with my investment adviser."

"Great. I should probably have one of those. A new truck like yours would be nice. For sure, I'll replace my falling-apart truck. I'm holding it together with luck and spit."

"You've made some memories in that truck." Linc chuckled, shaking his head. "I thought Mom would kill you when you came home with your first speeding ticket. So proud of yourself."

"She made me pay it off, too, by way of hard labor."

Linc chuckled at the memories, even if it hadn't been funny at the time. In fact, though Coop didn't know for sure, he'd bet Linc had helped his mother pay for the ticket. The one she'd made Coop pay off with her constant list of chores since he hadn't had a job at the time.

Linc was such a good big brother, who deserved every bit of success. As the oldest, he'd given up his dreams to help raise his siblings after their father took off. They'd struggled for years after Rick left. Linc had wanted to go to college but instead went straight to work after high school, to help their mother pay the bills.

Coop carried a heavy guilt because he'd always felt that it was his fault their father left, but Linc had probably suffered the most for it. As the oldest, Linc had sacrificed his ambitions for the sake of his siblings.

The weight of that guilt kept Coop from ever telling anyone what he as a child always believed he may have personally done to drive his father away. It was a secret too painful to discuss with family. Especially Linc.

His big brother could remind Coop all the live-long day he'd soon have his own inheritance, but secretly, he'd begun to wonder. What if news had gotten around that he was the brother who'd blow his entire inheritance? He'd told everyone that he would hit the Las Vegas slot machines or blackjack tables. The truth was that he'd always had dreams of owning his own ranch, but he hadn't told anyone but Alana.

They all expected good-time Coop, after all, and his dream had always seemed out of reach. It wouldn't completely surprise Coop to have the dream taken away. Maybe Wendell Fortune had skipped over the middle son who showed no signs of settling down and gone straight to Damon. Everybody loved Damon.

"Are you sure I'm going to get an inheritance?"

That made Linc stop fiddling with his complicated-looking remote control, and he turned to Cooper. "What makes your think you're not?"

"Don't know." Cooper shrugged. "Maybe I'm not the best brother of the lot?"

"It's not about being the best or the worst. You're a Fortune Maloney, my brother, and this is your birthright."

"The mines? Sometimes it's hard to believe."

"I know what you mean. It took a while to sink in for me, too. But I was the first to receive the money only because I'm the oldest. Until I got my inheritance, it wasn't real to me, either. Then, once I got the money, I had no idea what to do with it."

Linc spread out his hands to indicate the breadth of his newfound wealth. "Guess I figured it out. I didn't need a Ferrari, but this is a good compromise. And this way I can help others in the community. Does watching me and Max get our inheritance help you to believe it will happen to you?"

Coop snorted. He actually wasn't sure if it helped or hurt. It certainly woke up no small amount of jealousy for Linc, the eldest brother. The favored one. He'd been so perfect for so long. Their mother used to say to Coop, "Why can't you be more like Linc?"

To which Coop used to reply, "There's only one Lincoln Maloney, and thank God for that."

"It helps a little," Coop confessed.

"This is happening to you, brother." Linc clapped Coop's shoulder. "You're going to be a wealthy man."

"Someday."

"Soon. So, you and Alana?" Linc asked. "What's going on?"

Cooper shrugged. "I like her. If you want to know the truth, I think she's hot. I'm so into her—"

Linc held up a palm. "Whoa, whoa. Too much information, buddy. Remember, she used to work for me."

"Don't worry. Nothing's happened and nothing is going to happen. Didn't you date her, too, a long time ago?"

"One date, eons ago. We had zero chemistry. It was like kissing my sister."

"Uh, dude. Speaking of too much information… I don't want to hear another word."

Linc chuckled. "You *really* like her."

"Yeah, but it's very complicated. A big problem."

"She's not the complicated type."

The statement made Coop's stomach tense. What did Linc know, anyway? Coop was about to school his big brother.

"In this case it's more convoluted than you would ever believe."

"Why? What happened?"

"I like her, but I can't be with her as anything more than a friend."

"Ah, so you got friend zoned?"

"I kinda friend zoned myself."

Linc quirked a brow. "Any reason why?"

Coop didn't want to violate Alana's confidence in him, even if soon enough everyone in town would know. She was probably inside telling Remi now, who would then tell Linc.

Coop grabbed the remote from Linc and started flipping through channels, trying to find the rodeo.

"Don't want to tell me, do you?" Linc chuckled.

"I shouldn't."

"Well, if you really like her, I say go for it. You never know what could happen. I mean, look at me and Remi."

"No, it's not like you and Remi. You don't get it. This is different. It would just…never work between us."

"Never say never."

"In this case, I can."

"You look…worried." Linc took the remote back.

"I am."

Linc looked so puzzled that Coop wouldn't confide in him and silence stretched between them. His brother only wanted to help.

Finally, Coop broke.

"I'm sure she's inside telling Remi. The truth is, it's not going to be a secret much longer. It's probably okay if I tell you myself that Alana is pregnant."

"*What* did you just say?"

"She's pregnant." Coop rushed to shush his brother

before he could panic. "But you can't tell anyone else, okay? It's really Alana's news to share when she's ready."

"Oh, damn. What the hell are you going to *do*?" He hesitated. "You're not thinking of marrying her, are you?"

An unfamiliar anger burned in Cooper's gut. He'd expect this kind of response from some other bozos. Not from his big brother, the saint.

"It's not *my* baby," Coop said through a tight jaw. "She won't sleep with me. She didn't even want to tell me she was pregnant but tried to put me off, saying she wasn't the right kind of woman for me. Wouldn't tell me why. She finally confessed, maybe because I wouldn't go away. That loser Patrick O'Shaughnessy is the father, and he took off the moment he heard."

Linc blinked. "Damn. Poor Alana."

"Yeah. Sound familiar?"

"Unfortunately."

"I can't let her do this alone. She might not be the right woman for me but I'm going to be there for her. She's been abandoned, and all I can think of is our mom. How terrible it must have been to be pregnant, with four little kids, and have the father split. That's not a man."

"No, it sure isn't."

"I brought her here because she's going to need a whole army of emotional support. It starts today.

Remi is a good lady, and she'll help. And I'm going to be there for Alana. Not as her lover, but as her friend. I'm not going to be one of those men who walk away because this is too complicated."

A beat of silence passed between them.

"Sometime, when I wasn't looking, you grew up," Linc said, meeting his eyes. "And I'm proud of you."

Coop was proud of himself, too, because none of this had scared him off. He hadn't run the other way when Alana told him the truth. So though he might not be ready to be a father, he could and would be a good friend. That much he could do.

He wasn't sure if his desire to help had to do with how much he liked Alana—or the desire to be the very opposite of his father.

Alana listened to Remi talk about Lincoln for several minutes. They were getting along well, deeply in love, and Lincoln had recently asked Remi to move in with him.

Remi lowered her voice to a whisper. "And... I accidentally saw a receipt."

"For? A trip to Italy? Paris?"

"From a jewelry store." Remi clutched Alana's hands. "I suspect a ring, not just because of all the zeros in the price, but because he's been dropping hints."

Alana squealed, then covered her mouth. "This is amazing!"

Alana was thrilled for Remi, who almost hadn't had the confidence to go after Lincoln. She loved seeing a happy ending for her friend.

"I know! I'm the luckiest woman in the world."

"Can you believe this is happening to you? You and Linc, more than friends now, after so long. Does it feel like a dream?"

"Every morning when I wake up next to him, I want to pinch myself."

"What about every night? What do you want to do then?" Alana winked, feeling a bit of her old self coming back.

Remi bit her lower lip shyly, holding back a smile. "He's the most incredible lover. When he—"

"Okay, I'm going to have to stop you right here. I might get a bit too jealous if you keep going." Alana chuckled.

"Okay, let me show you our home."

After a tour of each of the four bedrooms, including the gargantuan main bedroom with a separate fireplace, Alana felt like a pauper. Rich people sure had a lot of room. She wondered what she would do with all this space. It seemed as if Remi had everything she'd ever wanted and then some. Linc had spoiled her with a brand-new wardrobe and her own car. But Remi was proudest of the library. Floor-to-ceiling shelves covered each wall. Alana was surprised to find that it wasn't filled with books yet.

"We're still decorating, and I haven't moved in all my books. They're still in storage."

"You could almost open a second bookstore right here." Alana turned in a circle in the middle of the room.

It was good to see that Linc wasn't just an amazing boss and friend, he was also a good boyfriend. Remi's dream had always been to have a bookstore, and after Linc came into his money, he purchased the old hardware store in town. They'd been renovating for a grand opening next month. It would be called Remi's Reads, a culmination of her dream after the book department she'd managed was cut from GreatStore.

"That's true," Remi chuckled. "I'll keep my special collections that are not for sale in here. One-of-a-kind first-edition stuff and some of my signed books."

"See what happens when you put yourself out there?"

"You were right. I needed to stop reading long enough to fall in love. And it's been wonderful since the moment I took a chance with Linc."

"I can see. You look so happy."

Remi blushed. "So, what's new with you since we last talked?"

"I don't even know where to start." Alana slid

her finger down the spine of a book. "For starters, I'm pregnant."

Remi simply gaped and didn't say a word, so Alana kept talking.

"The father isn't in the picture." She told Remi about Patrick and how he'd left town the moment she told him about the baby. "Nice guy, right? But that's okay—better for him to leave now than later."

"Oh, Alana. I'm so sorry."

"Don't be. I'm going to be a mother. Sure, it's not at all the way I planned. I was supposed to be married to the father when I got pregnant, and we would raise the baby together. I'd be a full-time mom, classroom mom, PTA mom, head of the car pool, etc. But hey, the best-laid plans…"

"But…you're happy about this?"

"Yes, I'm happy."

Remi drew Alana into her arms. "Then I'm happy for you, honey. Congratulations."

"Thank you. I wish the father had been as happy as you are about this." Alana snorted.

"It's just not fair the way a man can take off and leave it all to the woman. You need his financial support if nothing else."

"It would help, that's for sure. But I'd need to find him first."

"What are you going to do? Will your parents help?"

They probably would when Alana told them, or

at least when they got over the shock, so Alana fudged the truth. "Oh, sure. You know, they're excited to be grandparents."

"I'm sure they are. Well, this is going to be great. And you and Cooper seem to be getting along."

"We're just friends. I honestly think he's trying to be supportive since I told him."

"Really? Is that all? Because the looks you were giving each other… I mean, he had his hand low on your back and the way he smiled at you…he seems to be into you in a big way."

"We have great chemistry, but what can you do? It's not going to go anywhere. I think our budding romance was cut off at the pass. I'm not terribly sexy pregnant with another man's baby."

Remi's gaze swept over Alana's body. "I just thought you'd gained weight. But no wonder you're not showing off your great figure anymore. You're covering it all up now."

"I have a little potbelly." Alana lowered her hand to her stomach and pulled back the concealing sweater jacket she'd worn today, showing a small baby bump.

"You are starting to show," Remi said. Then she shook her head. "You're right, though. It's probably not the best time for a new romance."

"Tell me about it."

"On the other hand, weren't you the one who told me I should go after Linc if he's the one I wanted?

And to have a little more confidence in myself?" Remi put her hand on her hip. "How about taking your own advice?"

Remi had a point.

"But this is different. I can't take risks thinking only of myself and what I want. But sure, whether I have a boy or a girl, it would be nice for my baby to have a father. A man with solid character."

"Coop could be that man."

"He could, but he's not ready to be a father. I heard him say so before I told him I was pregnant."

Remi's face fell. "I'm sure it is asking a lot. And Coop has always been such a free spirit. I can see why he might not be ready for a while."

And on that sad note, Alana changed the subject.

"Hey, I'm going to need a list of all the books you recommend, especially those Harry Potter books you like so much. And the Narnia books. I heard you can start reading to your baby in utero, and I want to start early."

"Good for you. I'll put together a list. And if you order them from Remi's Reads, you'll get a discount."

"That's not necessary. I want to support you. At full price."

Remi elbowed Alana. "We need to get together again soon, without the guys. I'll drop by Great-Store sometime and we can go to lunch."

"I'd like that. You're my only friend who doesn't

just like to go out and get hammered. That life is over for me."

"What about Sari?"

"Yeah." Alana cleared her throat. "She's cool. I'm about to have a lot in common with her."

"Who's ready for some burgers?" Lincoln entered the open doors of the library, followed by Coop, ambling behind him, hands stuck in the pockets of his jeans.

He met Alana's eyes, a slow and easy grin on his face. A strong pull of lust squeezed in her belly. She'd never noticed how, beyond his good looks, Coop possessed an amazingly self-assured, easy but quiet confidence. She'd almost missed the wonder that was Cooper Fortune Maloney. He was the real deal.

And if it wasn't for her birthday money, and losing to Eliza's winning bid for Max, she might have missed him altogether.

## Chapter Eight

As he and Alana pulled away, Coop waved to Lincoln and Remi, who stood arm in arm at the top of the circular driveway.

It was surreal to see Linc, the big brother who'd believed he'd never settle down, already looking like one half of a married couple. Good for him, but holy God, in some ways Coop felt far more prepared to be a father than he did someone's *husband*. But poor Linc was in a love daze, rubbing Remi's arm, grinning, always touching her in one way or another. One thought kept running through Coop's mind: *What if Remi leaves him? What if she changes her mind about staying together, as in forever?* Money might be enough to get the interest of some women, but it wouldn't be enough to keep the *right* woman.

Remi might be the perfect woman for Linc, but you only had to look as far as his own parents to see that even when two people had been committed to each other for years, that could end suddenly. And without much of a warning. It could all be over in the time it took to get in a car and drive away to start a new life.

A huge chance to take on something as fickle and temporary as romantic love.

But when you became someone's father, when you created a child, that was *permanent*. Unchanging. And the love of a child was unconditional. Even if his father had never deserved it, Coop had loved him until the day he'd heard of his death. He'd been like a ghost dad after he left them, but his memory was everywhere for Coop.

He could see characteristics of Rick in all his siblings, who each looked at least a little like their father. He could see a few traits in himself, too, because Coop hadn't escaped the DNA lottery. You couldn't hide or outrun your family genes. Those genes, and biology, had proven to be financially beneficial in their case, if nothing else. But maybe because Coop was the reason his father had left the family, it was difficult not to feel the sting of blame surrounding his loss. If not for him, they could have possibly had more of a normal family. Whatever that meant.

As he drove, Coop reached for Alana's hand and squeezed it. "I hope you feel like you have more support now."

"I do. Remi is even going to make a list of books that I can start reading to the baby."

"The baby. I'm glad we can talk about this now." Turning onto the road, Coop spied a flyer hung from a wood fence on the side of the road. "Just remembered there's a Western show in town today. Want to go?"

Alana nodded, and he headed to the outskirts of town and the Cheyenne & Company Western Craft Show. Cooper had wanted to stop by the three-day event in Chatelaine at some point, and now it was a perfect excuse to be with Alana a little while longer.

As they walked through the lanes checking out all the vendor displays, Coop saw at least half a dozen people he recognized. Some from the Rusty Spur Ranch, and he nodded and waved to them, holding Alana's hand. He received double takes from a few of the women, one of whom Coop had dated in the past. It had now become a lot tougher to disguise Alana's swollen belly, when she was still small everywhere else. As the day warmed up, she'd removed the sweater she'd been wearing earlier. People probably thought the baby could be his, like Linc had for a moment, and Coop found he didn't care. Alana deserved this, to have someone hold her hand and walk proudly by her side. And screw Patrick for not being here to do it himself.

But it wasn't simply sympathy for Alana and her baby motivating Coop. If only that were the case, he'd probably feel better about this situation. He could be the good guy, like his older brother. Coop would be Linc Lite, doing the right and honorable thing, being a good friend. Unfortunately, this was not the case. He was still Coop Fortune Maloney, the daredevil, and a strong pull of attraction drew him toward Alana. Not smart. Risky. Distracting, too, because he couldn't help but think…inappropriate thoughts. Appropriate or not, no matter what Alana said or did, he had spicy and sensual thoughts. But how did a man romance a woman already pregnant with another man's child?

Maybe he should talk to Justine's husband, Stefan, about all this. Then again, Stefan was the father, and he'd be talking about Coop's *sister.* Nah, he couldn't go there. Coop would just need to figure this one out on his own. He'd simply continue to fight this attraction to her because anything else would mean taking unfair advantage.

They passed by displays of leather belts and purses with fine tooling, and men's and women's Western boots. There were Stetsons and straw hats of every color, shape and size. He checked out the price of a particularly flashy pair of boots he'd never wear on the ranch. But they might be nice at a wedding or other event. He might be attending one of those soon, given Linc and Remi moving in together.

The price tag on the boots nearly gave him heart failure. He'd forgotten these craft shows always added a zero or two to the price. Not the best place to find a deal. If Linc was correct, however, Coop would soon be able to afford all these zeros on the sales tag and then some. A sobering thought. But he no longer planned to waste all his money on careless stuff like parties in Cancún and Vegas. That was the Coop who didn't actually believe he'd receive the windfall. The one who thought someone would contest the will right before it came time for him to get his inheritance. Then, he could dream and fantasize all he wanted because none of it was real. But Linc, who'd never told Coop a lie, still believed he'd get his inheritance.

And if the will hadn't been contested yet, maybe it never would be.

Coop stopped in his tracks when he came upon a display of Western wear for babies. Little pearl-button shirts and tiny Wranglers. What a hoot.

"Who knew they made these so small?" He picked up a pair of Western boots, and look at that, the price tag had one less zero. This was in his price range.

"They make everything for babies. You'd be surprised," Alana said, picking up a tiny hat. "Cute."

"Great, I'll take one of each." Coop picked up a pair of little boots and matching straw hat. He threw in a shirt and jeans to complete the outfit.

"Good choices, Daddy," the clerk said, ringing him up, and putting the purchases in a bag.

Coop blinked at the comment, but it was a natural assumption to make of a man walking hand in hand with a pregnant woman.

"Those are so cute. Little Morgan is going to love looking like a cowboy, but you should have bought a bigger size. Isn't he around seventeen months now?"

"They're not for Morgan. They're for your baby." He handed over the bag. "In case you have a boy, but honestly, I think even a girl should be able to wear these."

"Coop, no. You don't have to—"

"Please. Let me. Linc already bought himself a new house. Max has his money and is trying to spread it around, even to me. By the time I get my inheritance, everyone in my family will be taken care of. Let me just do this small thing for you and the baby."

Alana's expressive blue gaze slid from questioning into shock. Her eyes widened, then she lowered her chin and took the bag with the utmost care. It seemed no one had ever done anything this nice for her, and Coop felt his heart thud against his rib cage. He understood far too well what it was like to feel undeserving. He'd do anything for Alana to believe she didn't deserve to be abandoned.

"Oh, Coop," she said. "Thank you. This is our first gift. Even I haven't bought my baby anything yet."

"You're welcome," he said, chucking her lightly on the chin. "I'm honored to be the first."

Alana went up on tiptoes, her eyes shimmering, and hugged his neck. "You're something else."

"Yeah." He snorted, attempting to lighten the mood. "That's what they all say."

But then, with one hand, she tugged him farther down by his shirt collar and kissed him. It wasn't a light and tender kiss, but a deep and longing one, filled with joy, and pain, and everything in between. He deepened the kiss, and they stood, getting jostled by the folks kindly choosing to walk around them.

The way she'd kissed him set him on fire and felt like an invitation. She wanted more and so did he.

Eventually someone muttered, "Get a room already," and bumped into Coop's shoulder. That move pulled Coop out of the moment, and with his hand lowered around Alana's waist, he led her to an unoccupied bench.

"I'm sorry about that." Alana put the bag down and sat. "I lost my mind for a minute."

"Do me a favor and lose it again later?" He winked at her. "Want something to drink?"

"Sure."

"Be right back."

He stood in line, thinking about the kiss and how much he wanted to get her home and rip all her clothes off. But he would behave himself even if it went against his nature. He would take her cues. Let her rip *his* clothes off.

"That's Alana Searle," someone said from behind Coop. "Dude, can I just say I'm not surprised."

"The only shock is that she didn't get knocked up as a teenager." The companion snorted.

"Wonder who the father is. We all thought she got around—now there's actual proof."

This seemed rather hilarious to both idiots, who burst into laughter. Anger sliced through him, accompanied by guilt. Unfortunately, he'd once been one of the guys who thought Alana might be nothing more than a little temporary fun. Now he knew she was so much more than he, or anyone else in this town, realized.

Coop turned in line and glared at the men. They turned out to be some clowns who had been a few years behind him in school.

"What did you say?" Coop said through his tight jaw. "I don't think I heard right."

"Huh? Well, I... I..." the one with dark hair said. "Alana. She's always been easy. I mean, you know."

"Easy, huh? And what about the father? Would you also call him easy? You were wondering who the father is, right? What if I told you *I'm* the father? Why don't you mind your own damn business?"

Damn, Coop hadn't seen that coming. He was implying that he could be the father of Alana's baby. The strange part was it felt so natural. Let them all believe it and maybe they'd think twice about talking trash about Alana.

One of the guys raised his hands, palms out. "Okay, then."

Coop not-so-accidentally shoved into the guy as

he got out of line. He'd lost all desire to get a drink or stick around this place a minute longer.

All he wanted to do was get Alana out of here before she overheard any other snide comments that might hurt her feelings.

The early-spring Texas day had turned bright and beautiful, a perfect time for the outdoors. Alana was glad they'd spent only part of the day with Remi and Lincoln.

The sweet gift for her baby was so generous that she'd nearly burst into tears. Had Coop bought her an expensive gift, she would have had to refuse it. But when he'd offered a gift for her baby, over-priced as it was, she couldn't refuse. She'd already decided she couldn't afford to be proud when it came to her child. Her child deserved every kind-ness even if she did not.

Alana had never been with a man this gener-ous and kind. The closest was having Lincoln as a boss, who'd been so concerned the first time he noticed her get sick at work the first few weeks of her pregnancy. They'd been in the middle of a conversation when she'd become so sick, she had to run. He'd followed her and waited just outside the employee bathroom with a wet paper towel. Of course, he'd assumed she had the flu and sent her home, ordering her to get some rest and not worry about work. Men like these Fortune Maloney brothers didn't come around often. She understood this more than most.

A woman sat on the bench next to Alana, her adorable black Labrador sitting on his haunches right next to her. He panted happily, and if Alana didn't know any better, she'd have to say he was smiling.

"He could go forever, but I need to take a load off," the lady said.

"He's so handsome. Hi, cutie. What's his name?" Alana held her palm out so the dog could sniff and check her out.

"Forrest. And I'm Mary." She appraised Alana. "Congratulations. How far along are you?"

Alana wished she hadn't ditched the sweater now. "Oh, um…thirteen weeks."

She kept forgetting she'd crossed into obvious territory. And if she didn't tell her parents soon, someone else from Chatelaine would. This lady wasn't from town—or at least Alana assumed so, since she didn't look familiar—so she wouldn't tell on Alana.

The lady looked over Alana's shoulder. "And here comes your husband now. Hoo boy, y'all are going to have a beautiful child."

"Oh, no, he's not…"

Lord, how she *wished* he was the father if not her husband. Coop would never abandon his child. Even if he didn't fall in love with her or want to marry her, he wouldn't just walk away from his duty. He'd do the right thing. They'd coparent their child. And while it would have been nice to have a man of character fall in love with her, the next best thing would have been a good father for her baby. At this point, she had neither.

Coop reached the bench, not carrying any drinks. He offered his hand to Alana.

She took it and stood. "Coop, check out this cute dog. This is Mary, and her dog's name is Forrest."

"Ma'am." He offered Mary a tight smile and tipped his hat. "Nice dog. C'mon, let's go, sweetheart."

"Okay." Alana picked up her bag. "Nice to meet y'all."

Coop tugged her along, his long strides so purposeful and steady he almost seemed…angry. She couldn't figure out what she'd done wrong, if anything. Lots of times her ex-boyfriends were upset if they found her having a conversation with another guy. She tended to be a little too friendly at times, simply because she wanted everyone to like her. Patrick, especially, hadn't liked it when she so much as said hello to an old guy friend. Ironic now. She'd never let that stop her from being herself, of course, thinking that if a guy was that paranoid, *he* had the problem.

But she'd been talking to a woman, not a guy. And Coop hadn't seemed like the jealous type.

"I thought you were in line for drinks," she said.

"Yeah, I decided we can just go to my house for

a drink." He held open the passenger door to his truck. "Is that okay?"

"Sure."

When he drove them out of the parking lot, Alana turned to him. "I thought maybe you were upset with me for a minute. You looked... I don't know...mad."

"Why would I be mad at *you*?" He glanced at her quickly, then went back to keeping his eyes on the road.

"I can't imagine. But something made you angry. Right?"

He hesitated a beat, giving her the answer. "Yeah. Some rude people I ran into."

Immediately she understood. Now that she was showing, everyone in town would have an opinion one way or the other about her condition. Her *situation*. And she had a feeling none of the thoughts or words would be positive.

"This is about me, isn't it?" She slid down in her seat, feeling small.

She'd love for Coop to be proud to be seen with her, but she also didn't want to cause him drama. With all the news of the inheritance coming to the Fortune Maloneys, people already assumed she was after Coop for his money. Shannon had only been the first to suggest it. Alana didn't care about the money even if, as a single mom, she probably should. She'd wanted to find a stand-up guy, and now that she had, the timing was all wrong.

Coop didn't answer but instead pulled his truck over to the side of the two-lane country road.

He turned to her, giving her his full attention.

"Listen, sweetheart, I don't care what other people think. My whole life has been about realizing how some people think they're superior to everyone else because they have more money, more education or a championship buckle on their belt. Remember, I grew up in a single-parent household. For years, I was a plain old Maloney with a deadbeat father. Now, all of a sudden I'm a Fortune and people see me in a different light. But I'm still the same cowboy I always was."

"And you don't deserve to be associated with me. People are going to start talkin all over Chatelaine. You're a Fortune now, and you have to think about these things. Appearances matter. People are going to see you differently. This is your chance to be someone better."

"I was *always* someone better."

With that, Coop unbuckled both his seat belt and hers and pulled her into his arms. Alana buried her face in his strong and powerful neck and the tears, coming far too easily these days, flowed again.

"Now you're with me, and no one will ever say another ugly word about you again. I swear it."

*You're with me.*

Alana wasn't sure what that meant, but it sounded so wonderful she didn't want to press any deeper. Still, a little honesty wouldn't hurt.

"You must know I haven't been an angel. I have a past. But I'm not nearly the kind of girl some people seem to think I am. Still, that doesn't mean I've been perfect."

"I know," Coop said, and his deep voice rumbled. "There was always something familiar about you. Something I recognized. Now I realize it's because you're a lot like me."

"Well, I think that's the nicest thing anyone's ever said to me."

Cooper took her face, framing it in his big hands. "I can do a lot better than that. This is new territory for me, but I like you. You're sweet, kind and so beautiful. You may be having someone else's child, but that doesn't change facts. I still want you to lose your mind again with me like you did earlier in front of everyone. I want to make love to you all night long."

She chuckled as a warm pull of desire went through her and she prepared to take one of the biggest risks of her life.

"Then let's get going."

## Chapter Nine

Alana held Coop's hand all the way back to his place, a rush of sweet anticipation tightening her skin. She wondered whether having sex now was too soon for them, because despite her previous three-date rule, everything had changed for her. Now, she only wished she'd asked Sari what to do. How did a single woman balance romance with a new man and impending motherhood?

But Sari had been married when she was pregnant by the father of her children. It wasn't at all the same thing. His sister, Justine, would be a better person to ask, but Alana didn't know her.

Still, she'd read pregnancy books that assumed a newly pregnant woman to already be in a healthy monogamous relationship. Regular sex was actually encouraged. But this would be her and Cooper's first time, and she longed for it to be special. Remarkable. She liked him so much, and she needed him to know this was different for her. Because, just like him, she was in a new arena.

The pregnancy hadn't scared him away. He'd had every opportunity to leave and never see her again. She'd given him the perfect excuse. Instead, he'd called and invited her to hang out with Lincoln and Remi. She hoped that meant something. In the back of her mind, a small part of her wondered if she was simply another conquest for Cooper. A more challenging one, to be sure.

But he certainly didn't make her feel that way.

He made her feel new. For someone who wasn't exactly virginal that said something. She couldn't wait to get inside and make sweet love to him.

Like hers, Coop's house was a modest two-bedroom ranch style, but the similarities ended there. He had a plot of land, and in the back, a small mother-in-law cottage stood separate from the main house. A small stable was situated between the two homes, with a fenced-in corral.

"I rent from Mrs. DiRiano, who's retired. It's a sweet deal for me, and the rental income helps her stay afloat and able to keep her horse in hay. I take care of Andy, too. Muck his stall, brush and shoe him. Exercise him in the corral. She can't ride as often as she used to."

They were greeted at the front door by a black-and-white border collie, barking a greeting.

"This is Laverne." Coop bent to give her a pat.

"What an interesting name for a dog." Alana offered her hand for Laverne to sniff. "She's very cute."

"I'll let her outside and be right back."

Coop's furniture was all brown leather, with a large flat screen hung on the wall serving as the centerpiece of the room. Decorations were sparse—an old horseshoe hung on one wall. There were a few family photos displayed here and there of him and his brothers, Justine in the center of all that testosterone. As an only child, Alana couldn't even imagine what it would be like to be raised with four big brothers as her protectors.

Coop served iced tea out of mason-style jars he may have been repurposing from old store-bought jams. The sweet tea he poured tasted delicious and perfect.

Like him.

He'd thrown off his hat, which she'd noticed somehow made him look younger. His thick, dark hair should never be covered by a hat, not even a cool cowboy one. They were standing in the living room after he'd served her iced tea.

"Do you like sweet tea? I just assumed you did. I mean the only other thing I have in here is cold beer and I know you can't have that. Would milk be better? For the um, the baby? I could run to the store."

"This is fine, and I love sweet tea."

"Are you sure?"

"Yes."

He was talking faster than normal and put away a few dishes on the rack while she drank her tea.

He didn't meet her eyes, seeming almost shy, and her heart squeezed as she came to a realization. Cooper Fortune Maloney might possibly be a little nervous to be alone with her in his home for the first time.

"So, what do you think of my lair?" He spread his arms. "Pretty amazing, right?"

"It suits you, but pretty soon this house will be the size of one your closets. And you deserve every inch."

His lips quirked as he canted his head and crossed his arms. "Every inch?"

Oops, she hadn't meant for that to have a double entendre, but looking into Coop's heated gaze, he'd taken it that way.

"Y-yes." She swallowed the rest of her tea and set the mason jar down. "Of space. Every inch of s-space."

*Now who's skittish?*

"C'mere," Coop said, and any nerves or hesitation seemed to have left him.

She went into his arms, tingling and trembling, feeling new as a baby kitten.

"Baby, you're shaking." Coop hugged her tight. "You don't need to be afraid, not with me."

"I'm not scared. Just a little…nervous."

"Me, too. But we don't have to do anything you're not ready to do." He leaned back, and the corner of his upper lip quirked in the start of a reassuring smile.

"You know I don't do casual, right? I have a three-date rule." She wanted to be clear about that before anything happened between them. "I don't think we should make any promises to each other, but while I'm with you, I'm with you. And only you."

"Ditto. This isn't one night for me, either. Not even close." His fingers encircled her neck till he rested his palms on her nape.

She pulled away enough to be able to read his expression. "I'm so attracted to you, and I want to be with you. If I seem nervous, I think it's because somehow this feels like the first time ever. I know it's strange."

"Not so strange." He brought her hand to his lips and placed a kiss on her palm, then another lower on the inside of her wrist. "I feel the same way."

She stroked the sharp beard stubble of his jaw. "You won't hurt me or the baby, you know. Physically, I mean. It's safe for me to have sex. The books encourage it."

"Good to know." Relief crossed his features. "I'll be gentle and slow."

"Hmm. I'm not sure how I feel about that. The gentle part, I mean. I can take it under advisement."

He gave her a slow smile. "How about I follow your lead?"

The suggestion enticed her. He groaned when she kissed his neck. When her fingers drifted under his button-down shirt to curl through the light hairs on his chest down to his abs, his muscles tensed.

She untucked his shirt, then slowly worked each button, one by one, never breaking eye contact. He shrugged it off his shoulders and let it drop to the floor. Yes, he was one delicious cowboy, and everything she'd pictured. Six-pack abs, a thin smattering of chest hair, muscular arms and biceps. She slid her hands down the hard planes and angles of his arms.

"What's this?" Her hand glided down to an old scar on his arm.

"I fell out of a tree. Long time ago."

There was no time to respond to that news, because he lowered his lips to meet hers, his mind clearly on other matters. He kissed her again and again, making his way down the column of her neck, nipping and tugging at her earlobe before his teeth lightly sank into it.

Alana moaned and clutched his shoulders. Her tongue traced a line from his neck down his pecs and to his abs. She felt him quiver under her touch.

"Bedroom."

She chuckled at his bossy tone. He picked her up

in his arms as he had the other night. She vaguely remembered the moment, since he'd woken her from a deep sleep. But now, she focused on his swift and smooth movements, carrying her as if she were lighter than a piece of paper.

In the bedroom, he shucked his boots and jeans, then helped take off her blouse. He moved with slow, deep, languid, wet kisses, lowering the strap of her bra, kissing bare skin. Her body buzzed with desire, his light beard stubble sending a curl of heat straight through her. His mouth followed a trail from her shoulder and up the column of her neck to her earlobe.

*How about I follow your lead?* She remembered his words. And right now she needed to tell him what she wanted. She wanted him. "I have too many clothes on."

He helped her unbutton and remove her jeans, and in seconds, she stood before him, nearly naked.

"Look at you. You're beautiful." His fingers traced from the curve of her waist to her hips.

In one easy move, he unsnapped her bra, then lowered her panties and helped her step out of them. She could hardly stand the intense anticipation. The sweet newness of this moment as they discovered each other's bodies, taking their time. She touched him everywhere, squeezing his biceps, lowering her hands to his rigid buttocks.

Coop's hands were busy, too, skimming down the small of her back and lower to cup and squeeze her behind. Those heavy-lidded dark eyes of his took her in, filled with a heady lust. He kissed her again, a long and deep kiss, his tongue curling around hers, warm and insistent. She threaded her fingers through his hair, kissing him over and over again. They were both breathless when he broke the kiss.

In a way, she thought he could be moving extra slow due to her condition, and she didn't want him to hold back. Not for any reason. She wanted all of him.

"Coop?"

"Yeah?" He looked at her from under hooded eyelids, his hand lowering to rest on her bare behind.

"Make love to me."

He smiled wickedly and then lowered her to the bed.

The pads of her fingers stroked the warm hard planes of his chest, and she could feel the pulsing thud of his heartbeat. Strong and fast.

He had a scar over one of his pecs, a half-moon shape.

"What happened here?" She traced the edge.

"That's an old one, when I fell off my bicycle trying to learn how to do wheelies."

She smiled at the memory of young Coop and kissed his scar. "Stitches?"

"Just a few." His hands glided up and down her legs. "So soft. Are my hands too rough?"

"Perfect." She framed his face. "You're perfect."

He grinned slowly, then kissed the inside of each of her wrists, removing them from his face. Lowering his head, he went down her body, kissing and suckling at her breasts until she nearly came apart. She wrapped her legs around him, urging him closer.

"Coop. I'm not fragile. You're not going to hurt me."

"Yeah?"

It seemed to be what he needed to hear.

She gasped when he finally pushed inside her, deep inside her, the delicious heat of him creating waves of pleasure almost too intense to bear. He drove into her, slowly and methodically creating a rhythm which rocked her to the core.

But she felt him holding back, a mask of concentration on his stony face. He still hadn't let go.

She lifted her leg higher, and he went even deeper. Coop groaned then, seeming to lose some control, and his thrusts became harder and more urgent. He was driving her out of her mind and out of her body.

She gripped his shoulder as every deep and powerful thrust drilled deeper into her heart.

Cooper was a goner. Tonight, Alana made him wonder if he'd ever actually truly been *intimate* with anyone before her. Well, he realized he'd had plenty of sex, but after this, he felt changed. Alana had given him everything. She'd opened herself up and given as good as she got. This in itself was a rarity for him. Satisfaction had never been easy for him to achieve, but right now, he could die a happy man.

"That was amazing." He tilted her chin to meet his gaze. "You're okay?"

"Hmm," she murmured. "More than okay. Fantastic."

"I agree with your assessment."

But no matter what she'd said, he had worried about physically hurting her. About taking her too hard and too deep. Instead, she'd been the one to egg him on with sweet and sexy words that drove him into a near frenzy.

They were quiet for a few minutes as he tried to resume the natural pattern of his breathing. Alana's head was nestled in the crook of his neck, and she felt perfect there.

"When are you going to take me home?" she asked him.

"Why? You want to go home?"

"I don't have to work until tomorrow afternoon. But I thought…maybe you wouldn't want me to sleep over."

She sounded tentative and insecure, and his chest pinched. And while it was true he didn't normally host sleepovers, no way was he getting rid of Alana.

"I want you to stay. All night if you can."

"Oh, yeah? And what are you like to sleep with? Do you snore?"

"I guess you'll find out, won't you?" He went up on his elbow, his hand drifting under the sheet to glide up and down her bare, silky skin.

"I talk in my sleep." She studied him from under hooded eyelids. "I've been told."

"Well, why didn't you say so?" He reached for his phone. "I'll record you."

She laughed and smacked his hand. "You will not."

"Don't you want to know what you have to say?"

"Not really. It could be embarrassing. If you hear anything, don't listen to me. I doubt I mean anything I say when I'm dreaming."

"Lucky for you, I sleep like the dead."

But she had him wondering. If she mentioned loser Patrick in her sleep, he might wake her up to get her to stop talking. Coop's goal was for her to forget the guy who'd abandoned her ever existed.

"That's perfect. Then I won't bother you." She smiled and straddled him, then lowered her head to brush a kiss across his lips.

He loved this, the way she so self-assuredly moved with him. They were perfectly in sync, as if they'd been doing this for years instead of a few hours. He had worried she'd be shy with him because of her changing body, but if so, she didn't show it. And he found her body gorgeous, her breasts rosy and incredibly responsive to his every touch.

Later, she fell asleep in his arms.

Coop didn't know what time it was when he heard a soft voice that woke him out of his sound slumber. He usually slept soundly, but he also never spent the night with a woman. So there were possibly a few things he didn't even know about himself. He'd just discovered something new: he was apparently in tune to Alana's voice to the point where it had ripped him out of a dream.

He opened one eye to see Alana had rolled out of his arms and now slept on her side with one leg thrown over a pillow.

"Size small. Pink, blue, yellow, tan, orange. Medium. Pink, blue, yellow, tan, orange."

Wait. Was she *shopping* in her sleep?

"Thirty-two B, 34B, 36B. Strapless, push-up, underwire."

No, she was working. Working in her sleep. Damn, she was adorable.

"Alana," he said in his sleepy, raspy voice. "You're talking in your sleep, baby."

"Bras. Panties. Satin. Lace. Cotton. Silk."

Well, now he was getting a little turned on, so he really wanted her to stop talking. When he rolled her back into his arms, he tucked her in close, and she murmured something unintelligible. Then she sighed in her sleep, snuggled into him and didn't say another word.

Yeah, okay, he could do this. This was easy. So easy it scared him a little.

Where would they go from here? He didn't usually think about stuff like this. She was, however, having another man's child. He didn't know quite what to do about that, except he wanted to take care of her. He wanted to help. Maybe if he showed her how a man should treat his woman, she wouldn't rush back into Patrick's arms again should the idiot ever wise up.

If he did this right, Alana would never again consider involving herself with someone who didn't have her and her baby's best interests at heart.

Laverne scratched at his bedroom door, which woke Coop even before the sun did.

"All right, all right."

Beside him, Alana was asleep, so he got up quietly and made coffee before going out to feed Mrs. DiRiano's horse. Laverne followed him out, as was her way, doing victory laps on the acreage, barking and chasing a bee.

"Hey, Andy." He'd mucked the stall yesterday, so this morning he fed him grains and a little hay for a treat. "You're due for a little exercise soon. I've got a friend who might like to ride you. She's beautiful and sweet, and I need to put her on a gentle horse."

He fed Laverne, and after taking care of his chores for Mrs. DiRiano, Coop went inside to check on Alana. She was still sleeping soundly on her side. He wanted to wake her, but after their marathon lovemaking last night, she'd be worn out. Besides, the book he'd picked up at the library about pregnancy said that a mother-to-be needed more rest than normal.

He let her sleep, guzzled coffee and started making breakfast, sizzling bacon in the pan and cutting up potatoes. He always ate a hearty breakfast, and even if Alana wasn't a huge eater, there was her baby to think about. She was eating for two.

"Hmm. That smells good."

He turned to find Alana standing on the other side of the breakfast bar. And she...um, she was wearing nothing but his white T-shirt. Her hair was tousled and mussed, her lips pink and swollen, and he swallowed thickly.

He dropped the spatula, then bent to pick it up and rinse it off. "Are you hungry?"

"Yes, I'm always hungry lately."

"It's the baby. The books say you're going to have a bigger appetite for a while."

She canted her head. "The books?"

"I picked up a library book. What? Don't give me that look. I read."

"About *pregnancy*?"

"I want to know what you're going through." His back to her now, he flipped a piece of bacon.

"Oh, Coop. You're so sweet." Her arms came around him from behind, wrapping around his waist.

"Okay, hands off if you want to eat breakfast, because I'm two seconds away from having Alana over easy."

"Scrambled Alana? Hard-boiled Alana?" she teased.

With a restraint that should earn him an award, he walked her to the table. "After we eat, then we have dessert."

He served bacon, fried potatoes, flapjacks, scrambled eggs, grits and orange juice. For a couple of minutes there was little conversation as he ate and watched Alana eat. Every time she licked her finger after eating a piece of bacon, he lost another brain cell.

She did it again, then smiled at him. Blast it all, she knew exactly what she was doing.

"Have you always wanted to be a cowboy?"

He thought about it—even here in Chatelaine, there were not many other options for him. And he'd always wanted to stay in town near his family.

"I love animals, horses especially. Seemed like a natural transition."

"It's hard work. Backbreaking. Your brothers didn't go into the field. Why did you?"

"Good question. I'm different than anyone else in my family. Guess I've always been the outlier.

I'm the middle child, and sometimes I think I got loud just to be heard above my perfect brothers and angelic little sister. Anyway, I'm not afraid of hard work. I'd be miserable at a desk job. You couldn't pay me enough money to do that."

"Soon you'll have your own ranch and won't have to work as hard."

"That will be nice, if I ever get the money."

"Why? You don't think you will?"

"The old Martin fellow seems to be taking his sweet time about it. I admit I sometimes wonder if only *my* check will get lost in the mail."

"I guess it's possible. The whole thing seems really odd, doesn't it? Your entire family coming into money, but it's being disbursed slowly, one by one. But I know what you mean. If it were me, I'd think the same thing—they forgot about me. I have a feeling they won't, though. And even if they do, you'll have brothers with money. I'm sure Linc and Max would give you whatever you need."

"I wouldn't want to take any charity from them. That's their money. No matter what, I'll be fine."

"I know you will be."

Good to know Alana didn't care whether he ever got his check. Because ever since word got out that he was a Fortune and likely coming into some money, old girlfriends seemed to be coming out of left field. Shannon, who'd broken up with him because he was a lowly ranch hand, had bid on him at the auction. Suddenly she didn't seem to care that he liked to spend his time on a ranch.

"Tell me. What were your plans before you got pregnant? Any dreams you wanted to chase?"

She was quiet for a moment. "Okay, I'll tell you, but you can't laugh."

"Are you kidding? Why would I laugh?"

"It's pretty unrealistic, and it's tough to make a living unless you're really famous."

He chuckled. "Why? What do you want to be? A mime?"

"What are you *talking* about, Coop?" She canted her head.

"It looks really tough. And I bet a mime doesn't make much money. Have you ever thought about it? Who do they work for? It's a mystery."

She gave him a look.

"What? That would be a tough way to make a living."

"You're weird." She laughed.

"That's a given. What about an Old West gunslinger, like Annie Oakley? That's tough, too. Oh, wait. I got it! You want to—"

"I wanted to be a photojournalist and travel the world. You can laugh now."

Coop was so shocked he didn't have words. "You're serious?"

"I told you—very unrealistic. In junior high I fell in love with the theater. But in high school, I took a photography class, and I fell in love with that process. Composition, lighting. There's so much involved in a single frame. It's a slice of time you never get back, but it's forever preserved in a photo."

"Dreams are supposed to be big enough to be almost unreachable. If you love photography, don't give up."

"Maybe my dreams have changed." She leaned back and patted her stomach. "I've always wanted to have a child, but it wasn't supposed to happen this way. I always figured I'd be married first." She shrugged. "All of my friends from high school are already married and having kids. And here I am, unmarried. Knocked up. It's not going to look the same for me, but that's okay. I'll figure it out."

"I know you will."

"It's another long shot, but I'm trying to get Paul to bring a photo studio to GreatStore. Remember those iconic family photos? It's time to bring the throwback studios back. They're still popular in the big department stores in cities."

"Great idea." He drank the last of his coffee. "You know, you should post all your photos to Instagram."

"I already do." She reached for his phone where it sat on the table and handed it to him.

He unlocked it and gave it back to her.

After tapping the screen a few times, she handed the phone back to him. "That's me."

He scrolled through the photos of an account

named Life in Pictures. She'd taken amazing close-ups of flowers, in which you could see every detail of the petals and leaves. There were also pictures of colorful and artsy shoes, a gorgeous rainbow, a sunset. She'd posted the photo of Oreo from the day he'd taken her to the ranch. And one of him he wasn't aware she'd taken, his back to her, arms braced on a fence.

"These are really good. Look at that. You just got a new follower."

She looked away, almost shyly, and traced a circle on the tablecloth.

"Don't get me wrong. I'm probably never going to be famous or anything, but I can still enjoy my passion as a hobby. And I'm going to have a new subject in a few months. A tiny one."

"Maybe it's not cool, but being a mother is the toughest job you'll ever do. I think it's honorable."

"I know how important it is to be there for your kids, because sometimes I think that's how I got into trouble. I used to envy the kids who had brothers and sisters. And kids whose parents were able to work in the classroom, or go on our field trips, bring cupcakes. Both of my parents worked, and when they weren't working, they only paid attention to each other. I had way too much freedom."

This was something Coop understood on a bone-deep level. He'd grown up in a single-parent household where his mother had a difficult time handling four boys and one daughter. All the trouble Coop ever got into—and it had been plenty—happened when he had little to no supervision.

"What kind of trouble did you get into? You know most of what I've done. I've raced cars, jumped off cliffs and once I jumped off a friend's roof into the family pool. His mother nearly killed me."

Alana laughed. "I used to sneak out of the house after they'd gone to bed and my friends and I would meet boys in the park. Smoke, drink a beer or two. You know how it was. I had a lot of boyfriends when I was probably too young to know how to behave with them, and…now think I lost my virginity way too young. I mistook sex for love. I didn't know what that looked like, but it's what I was looking for."

Coop needed to touch her then, so he reached out to stroke her arm. "Do you have a plan for the baby yet?"

"I'm due for a raise at my next review, and I'm hoping it can cover the daycare rate at GreatStore. I'm grateful to have it there, but unless I get a good raise, affording it might be a stretch. I want to stay here in Chatclaine if I can, but I imagine my parents might want me to move to California so at least I have some emotional support. I think that's important. It takes a village and all that."

The thought of her leaving…well, he hadn't imagined it to be a possibility. He should have.

They were both quiet for a few seconds.

"When…when do you think that'll happen?" he asked her.

"I don't know. Not until I tell them, that's for sure."

"You *still* haven't? You think they'll be that upset?"

"I don't think any parent likes to hear this kind of news, but I was always a big disappointment to them. They thought I was too needy and wanted too much attention."

Coop remembered how tough it had been for Justine when she was pregnant before marriage. If Alana had to move back in with her parents, she might be going into a hostile environment. He didn't like the idea. Alana needed support, not judgment.

"You're right, it's not easy, but your parents will get over it."

He hoped.

"Like your mom did with Justine?"

"Yeah, my mother wasn't supportive at all in the beginning, and it was a tough time for Justine. So, I guess I understand why you're afraid to tell them."

"But your sister married the father of her baby."

"Stefan Mendoza. Eventually, yeah, she did."

The thought of Patrick showing up now, working it out with Alana…well, it didn't hold any appeal.

She pushed her eggs around on the plate. "I guess that's the ideal situation."

He liked the sound of that even less. "Do you *still* feel that you wouldn't get back together with Patrick if he showed up? For the sake of your baby?"

"If Patrick ever shows up again, all I want out of him is child support." The corners of her mouth were tight.

"You sure?"

"At first, I thought it might work out if we were to get married. Sure, I would have accepted a proposal from him. Not ideal, but we could have made it work. I wasn't prepared for how he'd react. It changed how I felt about him. He wasn't the man I thought he was."

The thought of her having come so close to marrying Patrick made Cooper a little sick to his stomach.

It didn't make sense because Coop *should* wish Patrick would come back and do the right thing by Alana and his baby.

But instead Coop found himself wishing that Patrick would stay away for good.

## Chapter Ten

Later that afternoon, Alana clocked in for her shift at GreatStore and went straight to the employees' locker room to find Sari.

She found Paul instead. "Any luck with your new apron? I can't keep making excuses for you. No one likes the purple apron. Sorry if it's not fashionable. You still have to wear it."

"Yes, I… Well, I do need to talk to you about that. Can we go to your office?"

He frowned and led her to Linc's old office—now his—in the back, shutting the door. "What's up? Please don't tell me you're quitting."

"No, I'm a loyal GreatStore employee, and I love working here."

Paul was sensitive about being compared to Linc, whom everyone here still adored.

"All right, good. But I can't give you a raise until it's your review time."

She shook her head, laughing at the thought, because she would indeed ask for a raise when the time came. If she was lucky, the raise would cover what she'd need to pay for daycare.

Alana hesitated, but there was no other way to say this other than to just come right out and say it. "I'm pregnant."

He simply stared at her, jaw slack.

"I didn't want anyone to know for a while, and I'm sorry to have kept it from you. I guess I'll need some time off in a few months. Not much—whatever is allowed."

And whatever she could afford.

"I hope there'll be room in the daycare for my little one," she added.

Of course, the daycare center wasn't free. The company had gone above and beyond to have it in the building, but the daycare workers had to be paid a reasonable rate. Every employee who used the facility had the fee taken straight from their paycheck. Alana was already feeling the pinch of living alone since Lucy left. She'd have to find another roommate, even if all her friends were married. If not, well…she'd have to move to California.

"Paul, would you please *say* something?"

He leaned forward. "Um, congratulations?"

"Yes. Thank you."

"You're happy about this. Good, good." He leaned back in his chair and pensively stroked his new goatee. "And the father?"

"He's no longer in the picture."

"Damn."

"It's okay. I'm lucky to have friends like Linc and Remi and coworkers like you and Sari."

"Well, if there's anything I can do to help, give me a yell. I mean, anytime. And yeah, we'll see what we can do about a nice raise come review time. You deserve it, Alana. You never call in sick, and all the customers rave about you."

"I'd be good in a photo studio, too, you know? I could take appointments, and if no one comes in that day, I'll work in another department."

"I hear you. Look, as I've said, I'll do everything I personally can to make that happen for you."

Her spirits buoyed, Alana left Paul's office and went to find Sari in the locker room. She was stuffing her lunch sack in the staff refrigerator.

"Hey, how are you? Feeling okay?"

Was she feeling okay? She thought back to last night. She had started something with Cooper, and even if she didn't think it could last or go anywhere long-term, she was going to enjoy every minute of it. He was just…amazing.

"I'm super. Paul said he's really going to push for the photo studio. And I finally told him I'm pregnant."

"Was he supportive?"

"Yes. A little shell-shocked, but yes. I'm so glad I told him."

"See? It's going to be okay. We're all part of your village."

"The thing is, I hope you can give me some advice about something else. See, I started a romantic relationship."

Sari quirked a brow. "You and Patrick reconciled?"

"Oh, hell no." She threw her hands up. "I met a man. A wonderful man."

Sari grinned. "Some women have all the luck."

"He knows I'm pregnant with another man's baby, and he's okay with it."

"Holy shiitake, you hit the man jackpot! Don't let him go, honey."

"Don't get too excited. It's not going to last or be a forever thing."

"But it isn't casual." Sari crossed her arms, wearing a big-sister expression that said, *it better not be casual.*

"No, of course not. I don't do casual, no matter what anyone says about me. We're…together. But as you can imagine, I don't think he'll stick around. I'm sure I'll be lovely when it comes time for swollen ankles and heartburn. Cravings. Not to mention labor pains."

"I guess it would be asking a lot from a guy, but if—"

"It's Coop. Cooper Fortune Maloney."

Sari gaped. "The guy you won at the auction?"

"Yes, it was one date, but then he asked me out again. And again. We have great chemistry."

"Oh, jeez. But Coop…doesn't he have a reputation?"

"You mean like I do?"

"I never listened or believed that about you. I know how some people can talk about women, and it's not fair."

"Then maybe you shouldn't believe the rumors about Coop, either."

"Okay, fair enough. But it's different for men. It *shouldn't* be, but it is." Sari stared pointedly at Alana's stomach. "You know it is."

"I'll take care of my baby. I told Coop I don't want any promises. We're just going to take it day by day. I've had enough of guys making promises they won't keep."

"It sounds like you've got it all worked out."

Alana snorted. "You know I don't. How can I? I have no idea what I'm doing here. I need to know how I'm supposed to date a guy when I'm pregnant. Assuming he sticks around, and that's a big leap, how do you *do* it all? Balance romance and being a good single mother?"

Sari let out a hearty laugh. "I have no idea. Do me a favor? When you figure it out, please let me know!"

\* \* \*

Two days later, Coop finished mending the last few feet of the fence in the east pasture, took off his hat and wiped a line of sweat from his brow. It was hotter than a hellcat today, unusual for spring, and yet a fierce storm was forecast for tonight.

He found some shade near the barn, tipped his hat and pulled out his phone. No message from Alana after the one she'd sent him yesterday with a thumbs-up emoji in response to his asking if she'd had a good day. Even though he hadn't been able to see her again since their amazing night together, he texted or phoned every day. God forbid she thought he was done with her. He wanted a repeat performance of their night together as soon as possible, but she'd been busy lately, working the late shift when he was off work. She'd had a doctor's appointment during the day, too, and those were all reasonable excuses to be apart, but Coop couldn't help worrying she would shut him out again.

They'd come so far since she'd told him the truth, and he didn't want to backtrack. It was okay to move slowly—he fully accepted that. But she also didn't want him to make any promises. This was probably for the best and he'd accepted that, too. He certainly couldn't make her any promises since he was far from ready to be a husband, let alone a father. Still, sometimes it seemed Alana had lost all hope. And she was too beautiful, too kind to think she didn't deserve a little romance just because she was pregnant.

Since he was already scrolling through his phone, he decided to call Justine. She was someone who'd once been in Alana's shoes. Even if she lived in Rambling Rose and couldn't just drop by easily, maybe she could call Alana and give her some well-meaning advice.

"Hey, sis. How's it going?"

"Busy with Morgan. He's a handful. Keeps waking us up off and on all night with the teething. Lord, I don't wish teething on anyone. Maybe someday he'll start sleeping through the night again."

Coop winced. "So, um, how are you and Stefan doing?"

"Great. Of course, we haven't had a date night since the last time Mom came up. We're about due."

"I'll come and babysit if you need me."

She snorted. "You? Why would you want to do that, Coop?"

*Trial by fire? See what I might be getting myself into?*

"Why wouldn't I?"

"Enjoy your freedom while you have it. Sooner or later some lucky girl is going to catch your eye, and before you know it, you'll be a family man. Don't rush it."

He winced. "Yeah, well, about that. I wanted your advice."

"Go ahead, shoot. If it's about the money, my advice to you is to just hold tight. Have faith. I bet your check is coming any day now."

"It's not about the money."

"Really? I would think you'd be chomping at the bit. You don't make much as a ranch hand, and this is going to be a game changer for you. For all of us. I mean, look at Linc."

"And Max."

Max had recently bought his dream house and was dating Eliza, albeit long-distance as she was working in San Antonio.

"What do you think Damon will do with all his money? Buy Chatelaine Bar and Grill so he can fire himself?" She chuckled. "Maybe open up a new place in town to give them some competition?"

"Probably."

"I'm sure you're going to have a huge party in Cancún with all your friends. Just please don't jump off a cliff into the ocean again. That last time nearly killed poor Mom. And I'm not sure your health insurance will transfer to Mexico."

"I'm going to buy a ranch."

He didn't know why no one had ever imagined he might want to own a spread like the one he'd worked on for years. But he had only himself to blame. He'd allowed everyone to think of him as the wildly bold daredevil cowboy who'd never met a challenge he didn't take. It had been easier than

admitting he had dreams and goals that were probably forever out of reach.

But not anymore.

"Coop, that's great! You're a natural, and I don't
know why I didn't think of that."

"No one has. Everyone thinks I'm the fun brother,
but y'all never see me slaving away over a broken
fence line or pulling a damn cow out of the mud.
It's hard work, but I love it."

"I'm sorry if I underestimated you."

Almost everyone had. It was gratifying to hear
Justine say those words out loud.

"What I really called about was something completely different. I'm dating someone, and she's
really… I don't know what you would call it. Uh,
special?"

He didn't have the right words for all the confusing emotions coursing through him. Intense attraction, sure. But it was…more. Larger. Wilder.
The feelings were all so new and a bit like being in
a foreign country without knowing the language.

"Ooooh! Are you in *love*?" Justine said in a sing-
song voice.

"Don't be ridiculous. She's just a great girl, and
I want to be there for her. I thought you might have
some advice for me. She's pregnant."

"Oh, no. Oh, I'm sorry, Coop. You're definitely
not ready for this."

"I love the way everyone assumes it's my baby.

Appreciate the compliment, but I don't work quite that fast. I *just* started dating her."

Silence on the other end of the line. He could almost hear Justine gaping the way Linc had.

"Hello?" When the silence went on, Coop wondered if he'd been disconnected.

"Still here. Guess I was kind of thrown back there for a minute. Um, yeah. That's…rough. Is the father in the picture at all?"

"No, and the way I look at it, he doesn't deserve to be anymore."

"Why not?"

"He walked out on her. When she told him about the baby, he just…left. Abandoned her."

"Oh, boy. I know how tough these situations are, but there's almost no way for a guy to come back from *that*."

"Yeah, well, and I remember how hard it was for you when you got pregnant with Morgan and Mom wasn't very supportive."

"I wouldn't wish that on anyone. Being pregnant and on my own was hard enough."

"At least she's come around. I just… I don't know, I want to do something for Alana and the baby. I don't know where to start."

"Wow. This girl must have really impressed you."

"I told you. She's special. Different. I've never met anyone like her. I've always known her, but in high school she was way too young for me. After that, I wanted to ask her out, but every time I saw her, she was with another guy. It never worked out."

"And now you have your chance."

"Exactly."

"Well, if you want to have a relationship with a pregnant woman, you have to be patient."

"Okay, patient. Got it."

"There's lots of confusing emotions and physical stuff going on. Hormones. And a lot of pride, too, if she's even thinking about doing this on her own. Family support is important, of course, and I hope she'll have that. Otherwise, just be there for her. Remind her she's not alone. It can feel really frightening at times to be facing this monumental lifestyle change alone."

Coop's chest pinched at the memory of Justine facing single motherhood without their mom's support. With her judgment. He hadn't realized how difficult it must have all been until he'd heard of Alana's pregnancy.

"And remember, too," Justine went on, "most women won't want a man to marry them purely out of obligation. That's how it was for me. I wanted to believe Stefan loved me before I'd agree to marry him. Having a baby together is not enough to make a healthy and long-lasting marriage. This applies whether you're the biological father or you're not. Only love can make a good marriage."

*Whoa!* "I didn't say I was going to offer to *marry* her."

"You didn't have to. I know you, and you're not any different than the rest of my brothers. You'll want to do the right thing by her. Now that you're going to be coming into some money, maybe you think the finances could help her and the baby. But you'll have to love her first. If you can't do that, then don't even think of asking her to marry you. It's not fair to either one of you."

Coop thanked his sister, then hung up and went back to work. Feeding the livestock was a hell of a lot easier than trying to figure out how to help Alana without falling in love with her.

Because he'd be willing to do anything for Alana, but love was asking for a little too much from this cowboy.

## *Chapter Eleven*

Late in the afternoon, Alana drove home from her doctor's appointment. She'd had an ultrasound and seen her baby's profile! It didn't even matter anymore that she'd watched alone, no baby daddy holding her hand like she'd always pictured. The entire moment was surreal, and she now understood how she could love someone she'd never met.

The doctor said everything was proceeding normally and on schedule. The baby was the right size for term. Alana had gained enough weight, and all her prenatal tests came back normal.

"Want to know the sex of your baby? It's pretty obvious if you're interested in my educated guess," the ultrasound technician had said.

"Yes." Alana wanted to be prepared for *everything*.

"I'm ninety-five percent sure it's a boy. Those are good odds."

Alana cried all the way home.

Happy tears, because the cowboy outfit from Cooper would be just right for her little man.

*Her boy.*

*Her son.*

She tried the thought on for size. Initially, she'd wanted a girl, because she understood that world. Raising a child without the father might, at least in theory, be easier with a daughter. But she'd been lying to herself. It would never be easy, because a daughter needed her father just as much as a boy did.

After her doctor's appointment, Alana went straight to work the evening shift. It was mostly uneventful, because Paul assigned her to the deli counter, and very few people shopped in the evenings. She busied herself by arranging food and taking photos of it, then posting to her account.

After work, she pulled up to her street just as the forecasted storm burst from the clouds in torrential sheets of rain. Wonderful.

Of course, her umbrella was in the house.

She was already failing at this parenting gig. What if she had her baby when this happened? She'd need to remember to bring an umbrella with her at all times. Keep one in the house and another in the car. But if this were to happen in some future scene, she'd run inside to get the umbrella and protect her baby. Would it be nice to have a husband inside waiting, or running out to hold the umbrella over them both? Sure, but not necessary. She was readjusting her expectations. Maybe it *was* possible she could do this on her own. Maybe she didn't need her white knight.

Her mother claimed Alana had unrealistic ideas from the romance novels she'd loved to read growing up. She'd warned Alana would get unfair expectations from those books, then a few minutes later proceeded to flirt, and later make out, with Alana's father. Alana knew *exactly* where she was getting those high expectations, and it wasn't from her books.

Coop's words were still echoing in her mind, and the next time she saw him, she wanted to let him know she'd told her parents about the baby. So, she'd go inside right now, phone her parents and finally inform them that not only was she having a baby, she was having a boy. This would make it real to them, and how could they be unhappy when they pictured a healthy grandson? They could start buying things in blue.

By the time Alana reached her front door, she was drenched. Now, she'd have to change before she called her parents. She wasn't stalling. No. Not her. She didn't like wearing wet clothes, which was completely understandable. Leaving a trail of water behind her, she wandered into the bedroom and removed her sopping blouse and skirt, wringing them out and hanging them on the towel rack. She changed into dry panties and a bra and tugged on boxer-style shorts and a loose top. Now she was ready to phone her parents.

Except she should wipe up the water first. Again, not stalling. This was a safety issue. She grabbed a towel and retraced her steps. When she bent low to wipe up a spot, she slipped in the water and landed on her butt. Holy hell, her lower back *hurt*. What about the baby? Did he feel that jarring movement, too? Surely there was enough cushioning, but it may have felt like a jolt in there. Her back hurt so much she was afraid to move, and instead she slid across the floor toward the purse she'd dropped near the front door.

Should she call 911? The doctor? The doctor's office wasn't open, but she could call the advice nurse. A few minutes later, still on her back, Alana was on the phone with the on-call nurse.

"So, you slipped and fell," the nurse repeated. "Are you okay?"

"I hurt my back, but otherwise I'm fine," Alana said from the floor. "I just want to make sure my baby is."

"The baby will likely be fine. I'm more worried about you. Have you iced your back yet?"

"Did you just say 'likely'? That's not good enough. I want to be sure."

"Are you feeling any cramping? Pain in the abdomen?"

"No, I've just got a sore back. Is it okay to move? Will it hurt the baby?"

"Your baby is protected. Remember, he's so small he's basically floating around in amniotic fluid. You haven't hurt your baby, so please don't worry. Just be sure to call back if you have any cramping or see any spotting. In the meantime, it's okay to move if you feel comfortable doing so. Stay off your feet as much as possible for a few hours and ice your back."

She'd already done something right, because she'd stayed off her feet since the moment it happened.

*See? I've got good instincts. I can do this.*

In her next impressive move, she called Coop.

He answered on the first ring. "Hey, darlin'. I was just thinking about you."

"Are you busy? Can you come over? I could use your help."

"I'll be right over."

Coop hung up without asking any other questions. If it were her, or anyone else, they'd want to know what happened, but he was coming over either way. A surge of warmth and affection for him curled around her heart.

He sounded eager, but she hoped he wouldn't be too disappointed to find her lying on her back in the middle of the floor, too afraid to move. Not exactly a sex kitten here.

"Come in," she called out when he briefly knocked on the door a few minutes later.

He shook his umbrella out and did a double take. "Jesus! What happened in here?"

"I slipped on a little water and hurt my back." She pointed to a spot on the floor. "Be careful."

Far from slipping, he swept her up in his arms and carried her to the couch.

"Are you okay?"

"I was told to take it easy for a few hours, and I've been too afraid to move."

His face went white. "Is the baby okay?"

How sweet of him to care, but this was Coop, so she shouldn't be surprised.

"The nurse said the baby will be fine. I called and told her what happened."

"Oh, good." He took off his hat, raked a hand through his damp hair, then plopped it back on. "Ice."

Alana watched as Coop rushed into her kitchen like he lived here, opened the freezer and gathered ice in a dish towel. Instead of offering her the ice, he sat beside her and gently placed her legs in his lap. He then eased the makeshift ice pack under her back.

"How's that?"

"A little cold. Perfect." Lying here, her legs in his lap, she was grateful that if she had to be wearing her boxer shorts, at least she'd a pedicure last month when Lucy had dragged her along. "You seem to know what you're doing. I hear you've got lots of personal experience with injuries."

"Oh, you heard that, did you? True story. Probably all of them."

"Lucy told me about the time you jumped off your friend's roof into the family swimming pool."

"Oh, yeah, that's right, she was there. Called me an idiot. Maybe she was right."

"Why did you do it?"

"A story old as time." He tipped his hat and winked. "My buddy Mark double dog dared me."

"It's a wonder you haven't given your poor mother heart palpitations."

"Oh, I have. Too many people in this town have loose lips."

She chuckled, and a quiet beat passed between them. "Coop, I have some news."

"Yeah?"

"I found out today that I'm having a boy."

"No kidding." He broke out in a wide smile, and his hand lightly brushed up and down her legs. "Congratulations."

"The cowboy outfit is going to be perfect. Thank you again." Her eyes went a little watery, and her voice broke.

"You're welcome again."

"I'm sorry if I'm not too much fun right now."

"What are you talkin' about? You're always fun."

"I'm sure." She snorted and rubbed her eyes. "It's so much fun to ice my back while I lay in my boxer shorts with my legs in your lap."

"Do you have any idea how long I've wanted to hang out with you?"

She came up on her elbows in surprise. "Really? When?"

"Um, every time I saw you. We went to school together, let's not forget, so pretty much every day there. But you were a little too young for me. Then when you got old enough, well…you were pretty busy in those days."

"I recall you being pretty busy as well." She eyed him, knowing two could play that game. "Jessica. Madison. Shannon. To name but a few of your many conquests."

"As with you, my reputation is greatly exaggerated. Not that I've done anything to discourage the rumors."

"No, I see why you wouldn't. All my girlfriends wanted to go out with you at one time or another. Lucy was the only one who did."

"Don't remind me." He scowled.

"Hey, now, you're talkin' about one of my best friends."

Sadly, this was true.

He winced. "Sorry, but she's kind of rude."

"There's no *kind of* about it." Alana hesitated a beat. "She suggested to me that first kiss you gave me after our auction date was a pity kiss."

Cooper jerked his neck back like he'd been slapped. "Are you serious?"

"Lucy isn't always a very nice person." She drew up her legs to her chest for a stretch. Her back already felt better.

"But she's your friend." Coop's rough and callused hands slid up and down her legs.

"I know. Lucy means well, she just doesn't have any filter. Later, she always apologizes."

"You can do better."

"Maybe, but when I was younger, I had a hard time making friends. And say whatever else you will about Lucy, she has *a lot* of self-confidence."

"I have to agree with you there."

"She didn't mind hanging out with me even if when we went out all the men approached me first. It didn't bother her at all. She just believed none of them were good enough for her, not the other way around. You have to admire that kind of—"

"Delusion?"

"Coop!" Alana laughed and playfully kicked him lightly. "Confidence, not delusion."

He grabbed her foot and held it firmly in his big hands. "Let's agree to disagree."

Thunder crackled outside, and the rain continued to splatter against the windows. She felt cozy and warm here with Coop.

"How's your back?" he asked her. "Anything I can get you?"

"I should probably just go to bed. Gosh, I'm such a party animal these days." She stretched and sat up, ready to give walking a try.

"As you wish." He picked her up again and started walking toward the bedroom.

"I'm sorry, did you just quote from *The Princess Bride*?"

"It was Justine's favorite movie growing up, and we watched it over and over again until I practically had it memorized."

"That's also one of my faves. Such a beautiful love story."

He blinked. "What are you talking about? It was about sword fighting and pirates."

She laughed and shook her head. "Oh my goodness, you're hopeless."

But when he set her down on the bed, he slid her a wicked grin. Aw, he was teasing her.

"I'm sorry you came out here for no good reason."

His hand slid up and down her leg. "I missed seeing you."

"You're too sweet. I keep thinking you're a figment of my imagination."

"Nope, I'm the real thing." He grinned and backed up toward the door as if to leave.

"Wait. It's still storming out there."

He cocked his head. "It's just a little water."

"You could stay with me a little while." She smoothed down the covers on the other side of the bed. "Otherwise, I'd be worried about you driving. It's my fault you're out in this weather."

"All right." He took off his jacket and toed off his boots. "It's true that my old truck could use new tires soon."

Alana clicked off her bedside lamp. Within seconds they were both under the covers, him pulling her back to his front. She couldn't recall the last time she'd spooned like this and knew for certain she never had while still clothed.

They were quiet for a few minutes, listening to the sounds of rushing wind, rain and thunder.

Coop settled in, his arm low on Alana's waist, holding her close. He'd lied about his tires. They were fine, but if she wanted him here during this thunderstorm, there was nowhere else he'd rather be.

"In case you didn't know," Coop said, very softly and near her earlobe, "you don't just talk in your sleep. You work in your sleep. Buy something for me from GreatStore tonight. Size large, in blue."

"Huh?" She turned her head back to face him.

"At first I thought you were shopping. But you were working. Organizing the ladies' lingerie department. 'Size small. Pink, blue, yellow, tan, orange.' That's what you were saying in your sleep the other night."

"Ugh." She shook her head. "That's embarrassing."

"No, it isn't. It's adorable."

"At least I didn't reveal any secrets."

"You have secrets to reveal?"

"Don't you?"

He waited a long beat. "Sure, I guess. I'm the reason my father left our family."

The words he'd thought would lodge in his throat like a stone, came out easily with Alana in his arms. She wouldn't judge him the way he judged himself. Still, his gut churned painfully as he remembered what he'd done to ruin his family.

"I'm sure that's not true. How can you believe that?"

"Easy. I was the little hellion. Linc was the perfect oldest son, Max right behind him. Damon was a cute little boy everybody loved. And Justine, well, she hadn't been born yet. I don't exactly blame my father, either. I was a tough kid. Later in school they diagnosed me with ADHD, which answered a lot of questions."

"You think he left just because you were hyperactive?"

"Nah, he left because I used to get into all his stuff and often break it. My dad was very private and clung to everything that belonged to him like he'd never see another one like it again. A screwdriver. A stupid hammer. His tools were his. Everything was his. Even as a four-year-old I understood to stay out of Daddy's things. But this one time I got it in my head I would help him in the shed. He'd been trying to paint this bench but never had any time for it. I grabbed a brush and a can of paint he'd left open—"

Alana drew in a sharp breath and tightened her hold on the arms he wrapped around her. "Oh, Coop."

"Yeah, I'll spare you the details. At least I didn't have to be rushed to the ER that night for stitches and another medical bill. But I got quite a bit of paint on his truck. Honestly, I was trying to help."

Late that night, after his mother had read to him and tucked him into bed, he'd listened to the regular argument from his parents when little ears were supposed to be in sleep mode.

*"My God, Kimberly, that kid! What are we going to do about him? He breaks everything!"*

*"You should care less about things and more*

*about your family. Can't you see Coop is trying to get your attention? Of all the boys, he has the biggest hero worship for you."*

*"Why can't he be more like Linc?"*

*"Because he's not Linc. Coop has his own personality. If only you'd spend more time with him, you'd see he's one of the most loving little boys you'll ever meet."*

"I never told this to anyone, not even Linc."

A tightness grew in his chest and his voice sounded hoarse and almost guttural. Unloading this in some ways felt freeing, in other ways far too painful.

Alana turned to face him fully. "Since we're in confession mode…"

"I knew it," Coop said. "You do have a secret."

"My parents weren't expecting me. Let's put it that way."

"Another accidental pregnancy?"

"You could say that, but with a twist. They were married ten years before they had me. I heard enough stories from others to put it all together, even if they tried to spare me the truth. Neither one of them had any intention of ever having children. I really think they didn't know what to do with me. It was always just the two of them in their own little world. They'd traveled together, seen the world and then come back to Chatelaine, Texas, after I was born. No more traveling for them. My parents are still madly in love with each other. I know they're lucky, and I'm lucky, too, to have their marriage as my standard."

"But it's intimidating. Like a high bar to reach."

"Exactly. I don't mean to complain. There are bigger problems. I know you probably wish your parents had stayed together. But in my family, I felt like an intruder. Like a second thought."

And she might have also felt abandoned when they moved away to California without her. He wondered if that, too, was an issue but didn't want to bring up more painful memories.

Coop caressed her chin, then pressed a kiss to her temple. She returned the action by giving him a chaste kiss on the lips. Then another, not quite as innocent.

"I take it your back is okay?" he whispered.

"Yes."

He removed every piece of clothing from her, kissing the soft, cool, bare skin as he went.

Rolling on top of her, he pinned her under him. "You are the sexiest, most beautiful woman. I have no idea how anyone in their right mind could ignore you."

Then he made love to her, having told her his biggest secret.

## Chapter Twelve

"It's always like this after a bad storm." Coop's boot slid a few inches into the thick mud outside Max's new property.

Max brought up his own muddy boot. "Damn! These cost me four hundred!"

Coop's neck jerked back. He must have heard wrong. "Four hundred what? Dollars?"

"Bought these on one of my trips to San Antonio. Eliza has good taste, but I should have realized these aren't the kind of boots I want to wear to the stable. Lost my head there for a minute."

Coop had almost forgotten how much time Max spent in San Antonio these days.

"Yeah." Coop shook his head, barely containing a laugh. He could hardly imagine he'd ever have that kind of money and was sure he'd be just as upset as Max for ruining a pair of boots that pricey. "Lucky thing it won't be hard for you to replace them."

A look resembling guilt flashed in Max's eyes. "I was going to buy you a pair, too. You want one? Or two?"

"Nah." Coop waved his hand dismissively. "I can buy my own boots. Now, let me take a look at these geldings and make sure they delivered what we ordered."

About a month ago, just around the time he'd found his dream woman, Max had purchased his dream home. His girlfriend, Eliza, had been his real estate agent. She now worked for her friend Reggie Vale at the Vale Real Estate Group in San Antonio. Max made frequent trips to the big city and for now it seemed to work for them.

And conveniently, before moving she'd led Max to this home on several acres of land just outside Chatelaine. It had a run-down stable Max had rebuilt. He wanted horses, too, so he'd turned to Coop for advice.

As they walked around back, Coop glanced at Max's property. "I thought you wanted a swimming pool and a tennis court. All you got was the stable."

"With room to grow." He pointed to the tractor and crew of men who were working on digging a massive hole for the pool.

"When's the basketball court going in?" Coop chuckled.

"Soon."

Together they walked to the corral where the horses had been delivered this morning. Coop had been to a well-known breeder with Max and given him much-needed advice. His brother didn't know as much about horses as Coop did. No one in his family did. He was the point person whenever there were any questions.

And Coop was happy to help. This afternoon the focus on work had helped clear his head. Because last night—damn, last night with Alana had been… incredible. He was still flying high. This morning at the crack of dawn, he'd left her with what he hoped were sweet memories of the most erotic moments in her life. When it came to her, he was insatiable.

Max set his mud-caked fancy tooled boot on a slat of the fenced corral and looked at the two horses. "I walked these two out here, but the rest are in the stable."

Having horses wasn't a cheap endeavor. Coop had instructed Max on a vaccination schedule, put him in touch with his favorite vet and insisted paperwork be provided on their most recent veterinary exams. He'd checked their teeth, size, age, colorings and markings. Max had purchased five of the best horses his money could buy. A good start.

"Are you going to hire a ranch hand?" Coop asked him. "You should exercise the horses daily. They're well trained—I made sure of that for you."

"As you know, I'm spending a lot of time driving to San Antonio to spend time with a certain lady. I probably should hire someone if you have any referrals."

"I'd offer to help, but the Rusty Spur keeps me busy enough."

"Nah, if anything, I just want you to enjoy these horses. What's mine is yours, bro." Max clapped Coop on the back.

A nice sentiment, but Coop realized everything around them was changing at roughly the speed of light. Nothing would ever be the same, and not just because of the inheritance, which would change everyone. Linc was living with Remi, and Max was newly in love. They were already tied up in their new lives, which was fine with Coop. Were he getting married or sitting on a pile of cash, he'd probably be doing the same.

But there were no longer visions of Las Vegas slot machines and beaches in Cancún. Instead, a vision of Alana came unbidden. His feelings for her were fierce and completely unplanned. Unfortunately, he still wasn't like his two older brothers, who seemed so ready to settle down. And unlike Linc and Max, he couldn't even offer financial security. Alana, more so than most, needed that sense of security money could provide. He could provide that for her in the near future—if his brothers were right and he'd get his inheritance soon.

They watched the horses in the corral for several minutes and then walked toward the stable. Coop had advised starting with quarter horse geldings, though Max had his eye on a beautiful paint mare. But even though Coop was a great negotiator, he couldn't agree on a fair price with her owner and told Max to walk away.

"Got a surprise for you." Max walked ahead of Coop, leading the way. "Don't be surprised when you see her. I couldn't resist."

Coop knew almost before he saw the paint mare with the beautiful white and brown markings. Max had overpaid the breeder. Which, of course, depended on who was buying. But for Max's purposes of fun and recreation, it hadn't made any sense. This was an excellent show horse and would be well worth breeding.

"You bought her. I told you, she was way overpriced."

"Dude, you said it yourself. She's perfect."

"And *overpriced*."

"For some people. Before I went back to get her, I did my due diligence. I may not know horses like you do, but I know financial planning and solid investments. I'm convinced she's a good one." Max grinned as he reached to pet the mare's white forelock.

Coop tried to imagine for a moment what it would be like to be able to afford such a beautiful horse. "Congratulations. She's from excellent stock."

The mare's father had run in the Kentucky Derby. You didn't get much better breeding. Young, healthy, strong—she could actually be raced if she were trained soon.

"I'm the one who should be saying congratulations." Max turned to Coop. "She's yours."

Coop wasn't sure he'd heard right. Life was coming at him from all angles these days.

"What do you mean, she's *mine*?"

"I bought her for you. A gift. I ask you, is there any better time to overpay for something than when it's a present for someone you love?"

Coop gaped. "Are you serious?"

"Yes! I saw how much you wanted this horse."

"I wanted her for you. She's perfect. And now you have her." In amazement, Coop stared at the seventeen-hand horse practically made for racing.

"No, now you have her. You can keep her here unless you want to stable her at the Rusty Spur."

"I can't accept her. Save your money. You're going to have a wife soon. Kids won't be far behind."

"Ha! I love Eliza, but I'm not rushing into anything. She's on the same page." Max put up his palm. "Let me do this. Linc paid off Mom's house. I got her a new car, and I want *you* to have this horse. You helped me find the others, and you're going to help me every time I have a question. Horses are something I've always wanted to own, but you're the one who really knows what he's talking about. You've been in the trenches."

Coop couldn't put into words how grateful he felt to be acknowledged for this. He'd always made less money than any of his brothers and had the most backbreaking job. Even though he loved what he did, ranch hand wasn't exactly an impressive title. It carried with it an equally unimpressive salary.

"I don't even know what to say except...thank you."

Max reached to fist-bump with Coop. "You're going to be a rich man yourself soon enough, and I'll always be grateful I got to give you something before you never need anything again."

"I'll keep her here for now, if you don't mind. If my check comes soon, I'll be able to buy land of my own. I've been meaning to ask Eliza to keep an eye out for me."

"I'll ask her to put you in touch with someone closer to home. She's going to continue to work in San Antonio for now."

"And how's that working for you? Long distance." Just the thought of Alana moving to California gave Coop a feeling of dread that he couldn't shake.

"It isn't easy. I miss the heck out of her, and I find myself taking random trips to see her. She tries to come down every other weekend, but being apart...it's tough. She has career goals, and I admire that. And hey, if you love someone, it's worth it. You work it out."

"Yeah."

But California was a hell of a lot farther than San Antonio. California wasn't a day trip. If Alana moved in with her parents, she and Coop would be over. She'd start her new life, meet someone new, get married and live her life. Without Coop.

Max broke into his depressing thoughts. "So, what are you going to name her?" He nodded toward the mare.

"That's easy." Coop turned to his brother with a smile. "Lucky."

It didn't escape Alana that she'd used the previous night's events to avoid phoning her parents.

*I'm the worst kind of chicken there is. What would Coop do?*

She already knew what he'd say: Do it! Do it now! But that's what any daredevil would say.

With Coop staying over all night, she'd been otherwise occupied. Doing stuff a whole lot more fun than listening to her parents' condemnation. When it came to that, she could wait. It would actually serve them right to be told by one of their Chatelaine friends. If they had really cared about Alana, they would have stayed in the town where they'd raised her instead of moving and pulling the world out from under her.

Yes, apparently she was a little bitter, something she hadn't quite acknowledged. Decisions about moving across the country should be made after taking input from every member of the family. But she hadn't even been consulted, just informed they were moving to San Diego. It might as well be the other side of the world to Alana.

It was true, she'd been a grown-up, but at eighteen, a baby one. She hadn't been prepared to be on her own, and her parents should have realized it. When kids went away to college, it was often with the support of their parents, and most times they came back home, even if only for a while. Alana didn't have a home when her parents sold the family one where she'd grown up. She'd been lost and aimless for a while.

She and Lucy had had a good time living together in the beginning, and then Lucy found Rocco.

After cleaning her little house and checking her Instagram account for new comments and follows, Alana had the strength to do the next best thing to phoning to tell her parents: calling Lucy. If she didn't yet feel prepared for her parents' wrath, she could now deal with her oldest friend. No doubt Lucy would be full of judgment and *I told you so*s. This would be Alana's preparation and a warm-up to the real deal.

When Lucy picked up the phone, Alana heard a toddler screaming in the background.

"Hello? Hello? Stop screaming, Uma. Mommy has a phone call!" Lucy screamed.

"Is this a bad time?" Alana worried whether she'd be heard over the cacophony.

A door shut, and the sounds were muffled.

"It's fine. I need to talk to an adult. Thank you for calling. God, Alana, this is so hard. I'm not very good at it, either. Yesterday I actually told Uma to shut up! I told a two-year-old to *shut up*. I'm a bad mommy!"

Alana had never heard Lucy sound so defeated. "You're pregnant. I'm sure it's extra hard now. Does Rocco help?"

"He helps when he can, but he gets to go to work every day. I'm stuck here."

"Don't say stuck. You don't mean it. Uma is a sweet girl."

"I know she is. It's my fault. I have no patience with her."

"It will get better."

"I have no idea when! I'm about to have another baby, how is this going to get any easier? Huh? I have something to confess, Alana! Sometimes I let Uma sleep with us."

"Right. The family bed. You swore you would never do that."

"Yeah, *Cosmo* says it kills the romance, but it's either that or I lose my mind. Seriously, it's like torture, this lack of sleep. I'll do anything. And by the way, she sleeps sideways. Her head toward me, her legs toward Rocco."

Alana winced. This wasn't a particularly inspirational talk. It would be so much worse without a partner.

"You should have said something. I can come over and babysit sometime. So you can get out of the house with some of the other moms."

"Oh, those superior so-called friends of mine? Everything they do is so perfect. One of them knits little booties in her spare time. It's all I can do to go to the bathroom by myself."

Her change of perspective was shocking. Finally, Lucy had been knocked off her high horse. Or Alana had peeked behind the curtain to the reality of marriage and family life.

"I wish there was something I could do."

"Maybe you could get me a job at GreatStore."

"Huh? Why would you—"

"They have a daycare there and I won't feel as guilty checking in on her. But I'd at least get to be with adults and get a break."

And *work*. It was scary that Lucy would consider employment a "break."

"Um…your paycheck will probably be gone by the time you pay daycare for two kids."

"You're right. It's just a thought." Lucy sighed. "If only I could be more like you."

"Like me? What are you talking about?"

"Our house was always clean because of you. I realize now I didn't help enough and I'm sorry."

More shock pulsed through Alana. She should have called sooner because maybe two people in this relationship had to work to be a better friend.

"I'm sure there's a lot more to being a mother than keeping a clean house. You're good at everything else, Lucy, especially showing your little girl how to believe in herself. Don't lose that trait."

"Thank you." Lucy sniffed. "What's new with you? I heard you and Coop are still dating. Word gets around. I can only imagine how much fun y'all must be having. Please, please, give me something about the adult world out there."

Not exactly what she'd planned. Alana went ahead and shared a few of the spicier details, because that's what Lucy lived for. Both before and after Rocco.

"Oh, I'm going to have to get Rocco to try that! Wow, Coop is sexy. On our date, ages ago, he took me home before ten o'clock."

"Actually, I called because I have some news. I'm sorry I didn't tell you earlier. Remember Patrick and how we broke up? He left after I told him I was pregnant."

Lucy gasped. "That little weasel!"

She then proceeded to call Patrick every four-letter word in the book, as if she'd been saving them up for a rainy day.

When she'd exhausted her vocabulary, Alana told her the latest news. "I had an ultrasound, and there's a ninety-five percent chance I'm having a boy."

Alana waited for the lecture about how difficult it would be to do this on her own. Lucy would sing Rocco's praises and explain how she'd never be able to function without him. She'd mention the security and safety of having a partner in the trenches with you. Then she'd rail about deadbeat dads some more when there was nothing Alana could do about that now.

"Oh my gawd, we're going to have our babies around the same time!" Lucy squealed. "Maybe I'll have a boy, too, and our kids will grow up together and be best friends, just like us!"

To say Alana was surprised would be an understatement. She happily listened to Lucy prattle on about how, if she was lucky enough to also have a boy, she'd hand his clothes down to Alana's baby. How Alana should be able to save a lot of money, too, because Lucy would give her the infant car seat, the bouncy seat, infant bath and a bunch of toys. The rest Alana would get in the huge baby shower she'd throw.

"And you know that suggestion box at Great-Store?" she continued, seemingly without taking a breath. "I've been putting in a request for a photo studio about once a month like clockwork. I got all my friends in the Mommy and Me group to do the same. We take it in shifts. One week Lupe submits, the next week Sherri, then I do and so on. All eight of us are relentless. You have to be when you're a mother. You'll see."

"Thank you. I appreciate the support."

"You're welcome. The photos you took at our wedding were amazing. My parents still talk about them."

Made ecstatic by the love and acceptance, Alana hung up and knew she should call her parents right away.

She was on a roll.

## Chapter Thirteen

"Max bought me a thoroughbred horse," Coop announced to his mother and Damon when he stopped by for dinner.

"What about me? Why didn't he get me a horse?" Damon said.

They were seated at his mother's oak dining table, a new one that either Linc or Max had purchased, no doubt. They were spoiling Kimberly in every way. But Coop missed the old, worn table with grooves. He'd once tried to carve his initials on the leg of the table and wound up cutting himself with the Swiss Army Knife, requiring stitches. He even missed the old chairs, one of which hadn't matched because it broke when Coop had tried to practice superhero jumps off it.

Yeah, safe to say he'd broken a lot of things in this home. And he would love to be the one able to replace them.

"He gave me the horse because I helped him with the breeder we work with on the ranch," Coop explained. "I guess it was a brotherly gift and very generous of him. I'm sure something is coming for you, too."

"I'd rather have my own money, thanks. You will tell me when you get your check, won't you?"

"Oh, you'll know when I get *my* check." Coop flashed him a wicked grin.

"Big party?"

"Sure, of course. To start. But it'll probably just be here in Chatelaine, to save on plane fare and stuff. Kind of like Linc did at the LC Club."

Even if he'd never be anything like his straitlaced and responsible oldest brother, he could take a cue from the smartest decisions he'd made.

"There aren't many places in town to have a big party unless you want to do a two point oh version of Linc's."

"Maybe I'll rent your bar for the night."

Their mother, Kimberly, set a blue-and-white platter in the middle of the table. "Dinner is served."

"What happened to the old platter?" Coop asked.

Otherwise known as one of the few things Coop had *not* broken. It was perfectly fine and dandy.

"Eliza saw these in San Antonio, and she treated me to a new set of china. Isn't it lovely?"

So, now *Eliza* was buying stuff for his mother? He wanted a chance to help his mother, the only parent who'd really taken time to care for him, to *love* him, before his brothers took care of everything she'd ever need.

"Wow, Ma, you sure are gettin' spoiled." Damon reached for the serving spoon and dished out some roast beef and vegetables onto his plate.

"If I've told y'all once, I've told y'all a thousand times. Save your money. I don't need anything but to simply watch as my children enjoy their rightful inheritance."

"Well, these two children can't give you anything fancy. When are *our* checks coming?" Damon said, echoing Coop's thoughts.

"That's why I wanted to have you two over for dinner."

Coop jerked at the statement. This would be where she told them that the money had dried up. There was nothing left for Coop, Damon and Justine.

Coop paused, fork halfway to his mouth, ready to hear the bad news.

Kimberly folded her cloth napkin and set it on her lap. "I've already talked to Justine about this. And—"

"There's no money left, is there?" Coop interrupted.

Just when he'd found a genuine and worthy purpose for his.

Kimberly turned to him. "Why would you say that?"

"Maybe because I don't have a check in my hands, and it's been a month since Max got his. What's the holdup, anyway?"

"Yeah, what's the holdup?" Damon said.

"Now, boys. I've spoken to Martin Smith, and he's told me your check is in the mail, Coop."

"Like I haven't heard that one before," Coop muttered.

"Oldest excuse in the book." Damon scowled.

"He is being somewhat secretive about this, I'll admit. I was concerned, and so I called him. Now I feel certain, and I wanted to pass that assurance over to you. There's no way any of you will be shorted. The way he tells it, the riches are so bountiful there's going to be plenty to go around and then some. You're all going to have more money than you ever dreamed of. And all because your no-account father is dead." She crossed herself. "May he rest in peace."

Coop's body relaxed for the first time in weeks, and a sense of relief rushed through him, sharp as glass.

"All right! Good deal! Pass the potatoes," Damon said. "I'm hungry now."

\* \* \*

Coop stayed to help clear the table after Damon left for a bartending shift.

"C'mon, I'll wash, you dry!" Mom said, as if she'd just announced they were having a party.

"Why? You have a brand-new dishwasher."

Her mortgage had not only been paid off by Linc but her home also upgraded. She had a state-of-the-art dishwasher in addition to the new table and dishes.

"I have to wash the plates before I put them in. Might as well do it the rest of the way."

She had a point.

"Besides, I love dishwater talk. Damon is gone, so we get to chat." She turned on the faucet and started filling the basin. "This is right where Justine shared she had a crush on her first boyfriend. She asked me all about protection and how to know if it's true love. If not for the fact she was busy drying dishes and didn't have to look at me, she would have been too embarrassed to ask. You kids don't know it, but we mothers have our tricks to get you to talk."

"Like windshield talk."

"Exactly."

On a car ride to basketball practice was the first time his mother told him about girls and how to respect them. She'd had to give that same talk to four sons. And the car was the perfect place because neither one of them had to look at each other. They simply stared out the windshield. His mother was an evil genius.

"So, tell me, honey, what's new in your world?" she asked happily, dipping a plate in the sudsy water.

He supposed there was no better time to mention it, and the added bonus was he couldn't see the expression in his mother's eyes.

"Working my butt off at the ranch. Went on my bachelor auction date. Alana won me, you probably heard."

"Oh, yes, how is she doing lately? I see her every now and then at GreatStore. She's always so cheerful, so helpful. In a way I'm glad she didn't follow her parents to California. I was worried for a while about her being on her own so young, but she seems to have done fine."

"She's very responsible. Like me, she's on a strict budget and buys economy everything."

"Well, that won't be you for much longer."

"So you say."

"How was the date? I hope you treated her well." She rinsed off a plate, handed it to him and picked up another.

"It was…a good date. Turns out, she's pregnant."

His mother dropped the plate into the suds. "W-what?"

"Ma! Be careful. This is your new dishware or whatever y'all call it."

"China." She turned to him, eyes wide. "Coop. You're not—"

"The whole point of dishwater time is you're not supposed to *look* at me." He slapped the towel on the counter. "And it's not my baby, okay? Jeez!"

She put her hand on her heart. "I'm happy to know all my talk didn't fall on utterly deaf ears."

"The father isn't in the picture. He took off like his ass was on fire. Stupid Patrick."

"Oh, the poor girl. She's facing a lifetime of struggle."

Coop hoped that was an exaggeration, because at least Alana would only have one child, not four with another on the way.

"We've become…" He chose his words carefully. "Close."

She quirked a brow. "Close? Does that mean what I think it means?"

"We're in a relationship."

"Be gentle with her feelings, son. Remember, I was once in her position. A woman in her situation needs security first and foremost. She doesn't need a man foolin' around with her heart and mind."

Coop would hope Alana had room for both security and romance.

"Justine would say only love and romance will do."

"Yes, our Justine is quite the idealist, isn't she? I'm glad it worked out for her and Stefan. But take it from someone who's had to raise five children mostly on her own—I would have much rather your father stuck around, whether he loved me or not. Love doesn't pay the bills. He had a responsibility to his children, and to me."

Coop didn't have the heart to confess now, after all this time, that his father had left them because of something he'd done. Or maybe all the things he'd broken. Anyway, his mother wouldn't see it that way through the thick lens of her undying love for her children. She'd insist the blame was on Rick, leaving because *he* wasn't a man of character the way she'd raised her sons to be.

She went on, jabbing her finger in the air. "You should help her track Patrick down. Make him marry her and provide for her and the child."

"Are you kidding me? That tool?"

"He should be talked into doing the right thing. And you never know, it might work out. Look at Justine and Stefan. They rediscovered each other and are happier than ever."

*But I don't want him to rediscover her.*

*Where does that leave me?*

"Stefan didn't abandon Justine. You can't compare the two situations."

She shook her head. "Not at all. Justine thought she'd cut loose at the bachelorette party in Miami. And she used a different name with Stefan so he couldn't even find her! But when they ran into each other in Rambling Rose and Stefan learned he had a son, he was intent on being a father to his child.

Justine…well. She had a wall around her heart, your sister." His mother shook her head. "But I'm glad she finally let him in. And look at them now. They're a family. And so happy."

"Completely different, mom. Stefan did the right thing. He knew he was meant to be Morgan's dad. Patrick ditched Alana. He made his choice."

"You should still try to find Patrick because maybe he'll change his mind. Of course, I'm traditional in every way. I think marriage is always the right answer. It's the honorable thing to do."

"I'm not going to look for Patrick. He took off, and that's his decision." Coop crossed his arms. "I doubt Alana even wants him anymore."

"You never know. Maybe you should step aside, Coop." Kimberly went back to the dishes and rinsed off the one she'd dropped into the suds, then handed it over to dry. "Alana needs security above all else. She should feel safe and cared for. Love is simply an added bonus, and we can't all be that fortunate."

Coop snorted. "I don't think Justine would agree."

"Justine is about to become a wealthy woman. You can't compare her situation to Alana's."

Mom was right about the distinction. Alana deserved the same kind of security that his own mother had wanted and, most of all, needed all those lean years.

"I really like this girl," Coop admitted. "And I don't want her to wind up with anyone else."

"Are you sure? You have to be certain when it

comes to a single mother. There can't be any wiggle room. You can't toy with her feelings. Poor Alana has already been through enough. If you can't be sure, then don't bother her anymore."

"I'm not playing around here." Coop went back to drying dishes. "This is different."

He'd never felt this way before, though, and it scared him, too, because he knew nothing in life was guaranteed. But now, excitement pumped through his veins, like it had before when he tried something particularly daring.

Because he knew exactly what he had to do.

That evening, Alana was bursting with the news she had for Coop. She would have the support she needed. Even Lucy was excited they would be parenting their children together. Both Sari and her boss knew the truth and were supportive. Before long, she might be working in a photo studio doing what she loved right in the place she felt most comfortable.

Alana had the village she would need. She might not have to move in with her parents after all. All she needed was a raise to afford the daycare center, and she'd continue to be frugal as she had for years.

Coop had texted saying he'd be dropping by after dinner and had something special to share. She'd texted back that she also had something to tell him, too.

When he arrived, looking all rugged and handsome, she jumped into his arms.

"Oh, Coop, I'm so happy to see you!"

His arms tightened around her, and he lowered her to the floor. His smile was slow and easy. But there was an expression in his eyes she'd never seen before. It was…fear? No, it couldn't be. Nothing scared daredevil Coop.

"I like getting this kind of response when I walk inside."

She took his hand and led him into the living room. Was it her imagination or was his hand a bit clammy and sweaty?

"We both have exciting news. Who wants to go first?" She sat on the couch, curling her legs under her.

He cleared his throat, sat next to her and hung his clasped hands between spread legs. "Normally, I'd say ladies first, but this is pretty important."

The crease between his eyebrows meant he had to be worried about something. Perhaps how she'd take the news he was about to share. But she didn't think he was breaking up with her, because he'd seemed so happy to see her.

This was…something else.

She waved her hand, trying simultaneously to dismiss her concerns. "Then you go first. My news can wait."

"First, hear me out. If you think about it, this makes all the sense in the world." He clasped and unclasped his hands, then turned to face her. "We should get married."

The world stopped. She heard a bird outside twittering then jumping from the tree branch. Colors were dull and hazy. Her blue curtains looked gray.

So, this was what it felt like to have no words. For a week, she'd been leaving people speechless, and now it was her turn.

She stared at him, uncomprehending, and then brilliantly said, "Huh?"

"We get along really well, both in there—" he threw a glance in the direction of her bedroom "—and everywhere else. We have a lot in common. We have a similar sense of humor. We like the same music and food. And you need someone who has your back. Patrick took off, and good damn riddance. *I'm* going to be here for you and the baby. You won't ever need anyone else."

"But—"

He held up a palm. "Let me finish. I know I don't have much to offer you right now, but whatever I have is yours. And, of course, I'm going to be coming into some money soon. I want to provide you and the baby the security you need. That every new mother and child need."

"Security?"

"Yeah, of course. Maybe you forgot my mother went through this. She was pregnant and abandoned when my father took off. She would have given anything to have someone come along and offer to take care of her and us kids. Instead, she struggled for years." He took her hand in his and brought it up to his lips for a kiss. "I don't want that kind of life for you."

"I don't want that for me, either."

How ironic that only a month or so earlier, at the bachelor auction, this was exactly what Alana had wanted—a white knight to swoop in and fix things for her. Ever since Patrick had left her, she'd wondered if maybe she could find someone else who would be emotionally supportive and protect her and her unborn child. Exactly the way Coop was now describing. And the Fortune Maloney brothers were the kind of men with character she'd wanted. She'd thought Max would be perfect but had no idea at the time he was already interested in Eliza. Coop hadn't seemed like a possibility because he was so wild and out of control. But she should have realized all along that you didn't grow up in the Maloney household without a deep understanding of how to be a stand-up man. Was this her dream come true?

Still, Coop hadn't said a word about *love*.

She took a breath and spoke on the exhale. "We haven't known each other for long."

"But it feels right, doesn't it?"

Forever with Coop? "Yes. It does." She squeezed his hand.

Delight pulsed through her. This day would go down in history as the best of days. Her good news was B-rated stuff compared to this moment. She'd always remember this moment.

He loved her. He must. He had to love her, or he wouldn't make this kind of long-term commitment.

"And I do care about you."

His words slapped her out of her fantasy in one loud thud. *Care.* He *cared* about her. Like he cared about horses and ranches. She'd been through enough relationships to know that a guy who "cared" about a girl was the kiss of death. It was usually the explanation before a breakup. She'd been on both the giving and receiving end of enough of them.

*I care about you, but I want to see other people. I'm not ready to settle down. I hope we can still be friends. Because I care about you.*

Friends cared about each other. Family cared about each other. She cared about her coworkers, for crying out loud! She cared about her elderly neighbor. But a man who'd proposed marriage wasn't supposed to simply *care* about her! He should be head over heels, dumbstruck *in love*. It should be an almost embarrassing kind of overwhelming love, in which a couple made each other the very center of each other's world. Nearly excluding everyone else around them because they were so sucked into each other.

Like her parents.

Her parents. Here they were again, in her head, messing with her expectations. Making them huge and unreachable. Maybe their kind of romantic love didn't come along every day and Alana should accept whatever she could get. It's what she'd been doing all along. But since her first date with Coop on the lakeside, she'd been changing, and not only physically. She could feel her heart changing, too.

No, marriage and the security it would provide wasn't enough. She wanted...more. She deserved more.

Coop was trying to do the right thing by her, but he didn't love her. He hadn't fallen in love. It was in that moment she had to acknowledge *she'd* fallen in love with Coop. She didn't *care* about Coop. She had a sucked-in sensation like she'd never experienced before. Like the world rotated only for the two of them.

Totally illogical.

Supremely embarrassing.

And sweeter than she could have ever imagined.

"What do you think?" Coop closed his eyes and pinched the bridge of his nose.

"I think...that's a nice offer."

"Yeah?"

"But I... I have to say no. Thanks, but no."

## Chapter Fourteen

Coop was surprised, and why wouldn't he be? Alana fully realized her situation was desperate. But if she had to, she'd move in with her parents. They wouldn't turn her away, even if they weren't thrilled by the prospect. She was strong and had options. It wasn't necessary to settle.

"I don't understand. Did I do something wrong?" He visibly tensed, straightening. "Okay, I realize I don't have a ring. I'll get one. It's just...the minute I realized I wanted to marry you, I had to run over and ask you. I didn't want to wait."

She'd learned Coop had a difficult time waiting for anything. Funny, she'd once been the same way, and she couldn't help but think offering her marriage was one of the biggest risks he'd ever take. But Coop was used to taking them. Sometimes they worked, and sometimes they didn't. It didn't matter to him because he was bold by nature. And he didn't have much to lose, because he didn't love her like she loved him.

"I know you like me, and I like you. But you're not supposed to marry the *like* of your life. You marry the love of your life." She threaded her fingers through his. "My parents taught me that. I used to make fun of them, and they embarrassed the heck out of me most of the time. But I want what they have. When I get married, I want a love that will last a lifetime. And you don't love me, Coop. In all the things you just said, you didn't once mention love. Being *in love*."

He blinked. "I didn't think that was important to you. You were going to marry Patrick if he asked you, for cryin' out loud. Did you love *him*?"

"No, but this obligation is his, not yours."

"I want it to be mine."

This was difficult, and she didn't know exactly how to put it without telling him the truth.

She took a deep breath. "I want more than a marriage that's done out of a sense of honor."

He looked truly stricken then, his eyes wide, forehead creased. "But I... I..."

"I know, Coop."

*Men don't fall in love with me.*

Especially not the best one of them all.

He stood and paced back and forth, going quiet for several beats of time. During those moments, Alana swore she heard the sound her own heart made when it shattered.

"Coop, you were the one who told me love only has to happen for me once. Only one good man has to fall in love with me. If it's the right man, he'll be all I ever need. And waiting is hard for me, too, but I have to be patient."

"But—"

"You don't have to say anything else. No excuses." She stood to join him. "You gave me hope that it's possible for me."

"Don't make it sound like all you have is a memory of me. We'll always be friends."

The words cut deeper than she would have thought possible. He wasn't trying to hurt her feelings with those words, but friendship would never be enough. Not anymore. Her heart ached like someone had sliced it open.

"Sure. Of course. We're still friends."

Now that she'd turned down his marriage proposal, they had nowhere else to go with this relationship. She should leave herself open to someone who might, someday, fall in love with her. And he should be able to find someone he could love the way she loved him.

She walked him to the front door, where they embraced for what might be the last time.

He bent low to whisper near her ear, the soft feel of his breath on her skin a sweet ache.

"'Bye, sweetheart."

Alana shut the door, pushing the tears back. No time to cry now. Time to put on her big-girl panties. She had things to do.

She walked slowly to her phone, dialed and had an answer on the second ring.

"Why haven't we heard from you?" her mom scolded. "You said you were going to come visit."

A gratifying sensation thrummed through Alana, because Mom sounded frustrated she hadn't heard from her. Maybe they hadn't been perfect parents; maybe they'd ignored her and had no idea how to deal with a difficult teenager. Maybe they'd failed to see that Alana's struggles in school made her give up trying.

But deep down, the most basic truth was that her parents really did love her.

"You know, Mom, you can call *me* sometimes, too."

"I know you're busy and you like your independence, so I always wait for you to call."

Well, that was an interesting tidbit of knowledge never previously shared. How about that. Maybe she'd inadvertently trained her parents.

"Here's the thing," she said. "Big news. I'm pregnant." This time, she didn't wait for a reaction. She knew by now there would be dead silence. "Before you ask, the father isn't in the picture. I'm going to raise this child on my own. Yeah, I know it's not perfect, but it's the way it has to be. I'm not going to marry someone who doesn't love me simply for the sake of tradition. For the sake of obligation. I deserve for a man to be head over heels in love with me."

Alana heard clicking in the background.

"Mom? Are you still there?"

"I'm getting airline tickets. We're coming to Chatelaine, and we'll just see about this young man. How dare he walk away from you! Wait until your father gets ahold of him! He'll wish he were dead."

Alana didn't know whether she had a morbid sense of humor or it was simply good to have been reinformed that her parents loved her, but either way, she smiled. Then she had to tell Mom the rest. She explained that Patrick was nowhere to be found and that she'd fallen in love for the first time in her life with a good man—one who was not the father of her baby.

"Coop asked me to marry him, even though I'm carrying another man's child. And I said no."

"Why not, honey? Cooper Fortune Maloney is a catch. And I know you had a crush on him back in high school. Don't try to deny it."

"That was a long time ago. And I rejected his proposal because he doesn't love me. I love him, but he doesn't love me back. Sure, he likes me. A lot. He's obviously a good man. But I want what you and Daddy have. I want to fall in love with my husband a little more each day. I want to stay in love forever. I want a love that will last a lifetime, and I know it can happen. It's real. I saw that love every day of my life growing up. And that's my relationship goal. My standard."

"Oh, honey," Mom said, and her voice broke.

And only then did Alana let the tears fall.

After leaving Alana, Coop sat in his truck for what felt like hours but might have only been minutes. He didn't understand what he'd done wrong. She didn't need love right now—she needed emotional and financial support. To his mind, she was the one being unreasonable, and there was only one real reason she'd turned him down.

He was not good enough to be the father of her child.

Where did a man go when he'd had his marriage proposal turned down flat? The local watering hole? The lake, to be alone and curse loudly at the rejection where no one else might hear him? The ranch for a ride on the wildest horse? Maybe he should go see Lucky, because at the moment he didn't feel lucky. All were good options, but none seemed to be big enough. He'd have to do them all at the same time to make a difference in this frame of mind.

He went home instead, opened a cold beer, then

sat on the couch with Laverne at his side and stared blankly into space. Didn't even bother to turn on the TV. He wouldn't be able to concentrate anyway. The way he'd left things with Alana, they were no longer going to see each other. Because if she didn't want to move forward with him, she should find someone else she could marry. It would be unfair to stand in the way of what she really needed. Not just someone solid and reliable, but a *father* for her baby and a real husband. A man who was ready to be all of those things and more. And while he'd been willing to take a leap for Alana, and only for her, the truth was he wasn't ready for any of it. He had too many things to work out first before he could be a family man.

The only thing that had always scared him more than falling in love was being a father. It must have shown. Maybe Coop wasn't fit to be anyone's father. And Alana, who he'd already established would be a wonderful mother, saw this clearly. He might have bought her the cute cowboy outfit at the show, but when it came to raising children, besides buying things, he had nothing. Zero. All he knew was what *not* to do. It wasn't enough. Before Alana, he'd imagined he'd have all the time in the world to figure this parenting gig out—right alongside the woman he loved. Because deep down, he'd always feared he'd screw up any kid, whether his own or someone else's.

Maybe now Alana would move to California to be closer to her parents. Coop could imagine how that would go as soon as she got up the nerve to tell them. They'd insist she be closer to them so they could help and be a part of their grandson's life. He might never see Alana again. Never have a chance to see her little baby boy, never have a chance to see her become a young mother. And some day, he expected, whether here or in California, she'd find a man who would be a better father to her son. The thought made the ache in his chest grow.

Sick of feeling sorry for himself, he fed and took Laverne out for a run, then hopped in his truck and headed to Max's to see Lucky.

It hadn't been long since he'd been gifted his very own horse, but it hit him then that he hadn't been back to see her. Sure, he'd been busy with work, but before Alana, Coop's mind was on horses pretty much 24/7. Since they'd started seeing each other, he hadn't been able to stop thinking about her. And that crazy kind of pull he'd felt to her since their first date meant she was the first thing he thought of when he woke in the morning and the last thing he thought of when he went to sleep at night.

Max's truck wasn't parked in its usual spot, meaning he'd probably headed to San Antonio for the weekend. Mom might have mentioned something about that at dinner, but Coop hadn't really been listening. He made his way to the covered stables where all the new geldings were housed. Coming through, he checked on all of them, leaving Lucky for last.

"Hey, girl."

Coop pressed his forehead against her forelock for a few moments, letting his mind rest and unwind. He hooked a lead to her bridle and walked her out of the stable. After he brushed her carefully and cleaned her shoes, he saddled her and led her outside. He warmed her up in the corral, standing in the middle with the lead while she circled him. She was a dream. A fully trained and well-behaved horse. She would have been better for Max, who didn't know horses the way Coop did. Some days Coop preferred to ride an untrained, just-this-side-of-unbroken horse. They seemed to understand each other best.

"But you and me…we'll get to know each other. I need to slow down anyway."

Mounting Lucky, he rode through the green pasture where the grass had hardened after the last rainstorm. Lucky responded to commands as Coop would have expected the daughter of a champion, and he pushed her to a trot, then a gallop. He rode like the wind, forgetting all his burdens. Forgetting his failures and his shame. Forgetting everything but the powerful fifteen-hundred-pound beast below him, responding to his every command.

*First you go with the horse, then the horse goes with you, then you go together.*

Words said by one of the greatest horse trainers of all time, Tom Dorrance.

He stopped at the crest of a small hill overlooking a creek and led Lucky to the water. Like Coop, Max had wanted more land than a house. The house needed work, and so did the stables, but the land was perfect.

Someday soon Coop, too, would have land, and horses, and everything he'd ever wanted.

But for the first time, he thought it might not be enough.

After cleaning Lucky's shoes of any bits of dirt and rock she'd caught on their ride, Coop unsaddled, brushed, fed and put her to rest. The ride had been invigorating, peaceful and transformative.

And now it was time to head over to Linc's.

It seemed once a year they discussed Rick and how his abandonment had affected them all. They'd been talking about him a lot more lately since Martin Smith showed up. Their father had screwed Linc's life up the most because, as the oldest son, he'd been left to feel responsible for them all. Coop had never apologized to his big brother for his part in ruining his life. He'd been too full of shame and regret.

Maybe now that money had eased his situation, Linc might be more forgiving of what Coop had to confess. Besides, Coop's heart already felt raw and torn. It couldn't get much worse for him.

When he arrived, Coop pounded on the door to the fortress where Linc and Remi lived. Now, he envied what they had. A quiet kind of love and passion for each other. Solid. They both loved and respected each other. The way it should be.

"Hey." Linc opened the door with a big smile.

"Can we talk?" Coop gestured with his chin. "Outside?"

Brow furrowed, Linc shut the door and followed Coop out. He walked to the edge of Linc's property, where he crossed his arms.

Sunlight was fading, the trees shadowed in a soft light.

"What's up?" Linc asked.

"Something important. I feel it's time you know the truth."

"About what?"

"About Dad. I'm sorry, Linc, I know it changed your entire life when he left us. I haven't wanted to mention this, because either way, it doesn't change a thing. You had to give up your dreams to help raise us."

"That's all in the past. Why are you bringing it up now?"

"Because I'm the reason he left us. If you think about it, we both know it's the truth. I was the wild one, the hyperactive little kid who broke everything.

I used to hear him at night, yelling to Mom that he didn't know how much longer he could put up with me. And the day he left, I'd tried to paint the bench in his shed, to help him. He'd complained he never had time for any of his projects. Just work, come home, dinner, deal with kids and sleep. Rinse and repeat the next day. I thought if I helped with the paint job he'd started and never had time to finish, he would stop being so unhappy all the time. I wound up spilling brown paint all over his truck."

"I remember that," Linc said, his scowl deep. "You were *four*, Coop. Four."

"And a hell of a lot to handle. One of me was like five of you for all the energy I took up. I remember when he found the spilled paint. He gave me a look of disgust, and then he turned and walked out. The next day he left for good. Never came back."

"And you think *that's* why?"

Coop shrugged. "That plus everything else I broke or ruined."

"You can't honestly believe you're responsible for the actions of a grown man. You don't leave your wife and kids because a four-year-old spills paint on your truck. You lock up your paint and shed when you don't want an overly inquisitive kid to get into your stuff. The reason our father left is because he wasn't a man of character like we've been raised to be. He was weak. Selfish. That's something you had nothing to do with."

Coop shook his head. He'd been carrying this weight around for so long that now, saying it out loud for only the second time, he realized how ridiculous it sounded. As a four-year-old, he'd been responsible for very little.

Linc kept talking. "My memories of you before Rick left are different. Actually, I remember you as the funny one, always making us laugh. One of the few times I saw our father laugh was when you ran around the house wearing a makeshift cape, holding up your fist, yelling, 'I'm Batman! I fight crime!'"

Coop chuckled at the memory. "Maybe you're right. Maybe I'm overreacting."

"You are." Linc clapped a hand on Coop's back. "What happened? Is this about our inheritance? Are you still worried about that?"

"No." Coop shook his head. "I asked Alana to marry me. She said no, and I'm sure it's because she realizes I wouldn't be a good father to her baby. Maybe she's right. I'm not ready to be a family man, but with her, I wanted to try."

Linc gasped, wheezed and hit his chest. "You *what*? You asked her to marry you?"

"That's right."

"How long have you been dating her? Two whole minutes?"

"Hey, look. You don't understand. She needs someone now. Safety and security. Mom suggested I go looking for the deadbeat dad. But Patrick isn't good enough for her, and why should I look for him when I'm right here, willing and able to take care of them both? I don't care that it's not my baby. It's her baby, and he deserves to grow up with a father."

"Wow." Linc slowly shook his head. "You *have* grown up, haven't you? I can't believe you're willing to marry her just to take care of her and the baby. That's a solid reason, but I wonder if it's enough to get married. I've resisted marriage for so long, and I'm really in love with Remi."

"Well, Alana said no, so I'm *not* getting married."

"I don't get it." Linc shook his head slowly. "How did you ask her? Did you make a big production out of it? Go down on bended knee, the whole bit?"

Coop pinched the bridge of his nose and winced. It was possible that in his hurry and excitement, he'd neglected a few things.

"I just ran right over when I realized I wanted to do this. We're right for each other. I told her I'd get her a ring later when the money comes in. Something big and flashy."

"And so, you told her you loved her and wanted to spend the rest of your life with her, and she said... what?"

"That's not exactly how it went." Coop cleared his throat.

Then he explained everything.

Lincoln gaped. "Let me get this straight. You told her you *cared* about her? Cared?"

Oh, damn. Yeah, wasn't that what he told a girl when he just wanted to be friends? It was what he'd told Shannon when he'd broken up with her.

*I really care about you, but I think we should see other people.*

Coop groaned and palmed his face. He'd been nervous and so excited that he'd bungled the whole thing.

A marriage proposal should be special and memorable. No wonder she hadn't accepted.

"Oh, man. I got this so wrong."

"Hang on, wait a minute here. Maybe there's some truth to what you said. Something you haven't clearly admitted even to yourself. Do you care about her, or are you in love with her?"

Since their first date, she'd been everything he thought about from the time he woke up to the time he fell asleep. It had all happened so fast he felt a little stunned. Confused. Like he was trying to keep up in a race and kept winding up a click or two behind no matter how fast he ran. He'd always believed love would quietly sneak up on him, not slam into him like a hammer on a nail.

But if he had to pin it down to one moment, one single moment when he'd fallen for her...it was probably when he bought her baby the small cowboy outfit. The look of genuine surprise in her eyes that someone had done something this nice for her…it was clear she'd never expected a thing from him. And for a moment, he'd been gratified. For once, he'd done something right. Then he'd experienced a jolt of awareness such as he'd never felt in his life. It was an emotion he'd struggled to name, a cross between excitement, tenderness and a quiet kind of certainty.

"I almost can't believe it, because it happened so fast. I didn't think that would ever happen to me like this. But yeah, I believe I'm in love with her."

"Sometimes that's how it goes."

"It hit me over the head like a two-by-four. She makes me feel that I can do anything. The way she looks at me…like I'm a brand-new Maserati or something."

Linc chuckled. "Well, you can't ask for any more than that. And how does she feel about you?"

"I don't know."

But when he thought about it, the way he often caught her studying him, the way she wanted more than a convenient arrangement, all pointed him in one direction. She might actually feel the same way he did, and wouldn't that be perfect? She wanted what her parents had, and so did he. He wanted to still walk hand in hand with his wife when they were in their fifties and beyond. He wanted to embarrass his children when he grabbed their mother in a fierce kiss.

"I think you should wait a couple of days and try again. This time, brother, do it up big. A huge romantic gesture. A *grand* gesture."

"Proposing is a big deal, and she shut me down. She's already rejected me once. I'm a little gun-shy now."

"You? Coop Fortune Maloney? Scared?" Linc tipped back on his heels. "I'm going to do something I've never done before, because our mother made me promise. But I believe she'd be okay with this one. I double dog dare you."

## Chapter Fifteen

After talking to her mother for an hour, Alana went to bed and cried herself to sleep. The ache had wrapped around her heart like a vise.

She'd talked her mother into waiting a little while to fly out to Chatelaine, assuring her she'd be okay. As suspected, they thought it best for Alana to move in with them. Her parents suggested a family meeting to discuss logistics and a timeline for the move. They talked up the great weather in California, the parks they lived near, a Montessori preschool and even offered to babysit. Their support was invaluable. Alana was a grown-up who'd been on her own for years, and she didn't want to regress. But the idea made sense, too. She didn't have a partner. They could be a little family again, and this time her parents would probably dote on her little boy.

The next day, she cried all the way to work, where she was pleasant to coworkers and cheerful with customers. She hadn't earned employee of the month several times in a row for nothing.

"Keep up the good work." Paul saluted cheerfully as he passed the deli counter. "Another compliment by a satisfied customer."

She held her arms out. "And I'm even wearing my new apron."

But it wasn't a new apron at all. Just the same old comfy one tied loosely over her expanding waistline. She was finally comfortable and relaxed to be obvious about her pregnancy.

"Thank you for that."

Next to Linc, Paul was the best boss she'd ever had. She'd miss him when she moved to San Diego. While she'd miss Coop most of all, she'd miss all the good people of Chatelaine, where she'd grown up and had deep roots. The thought brought fresh tears to her eyes.

A few customers had already asked whether she was pregnant. Hard to disguise with the bright purple apron tied around her waist, emphasizing her rounded belly. Everyone had good wishes for a healthy baby, which was nice. No one asked whether or not she would be getting married. Also nice.

But all the compliments and pleasantries couldn't

take away the pang of realizing she'd missed out on being with the best man she'd ever met. Her timing had always been off with men, and this was more of the same. Had she dated Coop first, she liked to think there never would have been a Patrick at all. Then a wave of guilt would hit her, because if not for Patrick, she might not be pregnant. And she already loved her little bean so much she'd do anything to keep him. Besides, if someone like Coop had come from a man like Rick Maloney, then anything was possible. It wasn't all simply left up to the DNA lottery.

A few times during her shift, she cheered herself out of the fresh, gaping hole in her heart by whipping out her phone and taking photos of elaborate displays of food. When the deli counter was slow, she artfully arranged a platter with sliced tomatoes drizzled in olive oil, a hunk of bread and olives scattered about here and there. She took photos, playing with lighting and filters, and posted to her Instagram page. Who knew, maybe someday she could get paid for taking pictures of food.

Come visit the deli counter today. Made from ingredients at GreatStore, she posted.

Within seconds, Coop had liked the photo. She swallowed the lump in her throat. She was going to miss her cowboy. He'd always made her feel so wanted and loved, whether he loved her or not.

Sari came up to the counter, her apron hanging around her neck and a plastic store bag in her hand. She'd obviously ended her shift but hadn't yet picked up the boys from the daycare upstairs.

"Hey there, what's healthy and on sale today?"

Like Alana, Sari only shopped the specials. But she also was a lot stricter than Alana on feeding her family healthy food. Pointing to the broccoli salad and creamy risotto, Alana loaded Sari up with what she assumed might be dinner tonight.

"I still can't believe your kids like broccoli."

"You'll have to see it in action. Want to come over for dinner tomorrow night?"

"Really? Sure, thank you."

"Oh, almost forgot." Sari reached inside the plastic bag. "Usually when I'm holding a bag it's something I got for the boys. These were on clearance, and I got them for your baby."

She held up a packet of blue-and-white onesies. "Boy or girl, this will work just fine."

"I found out I'm having a boy." A tear slipped down her cheek and Alana wiped it away, embarrassed by the emotion.

Sari squealed. "I'll have tons of hand-me-downs for you."

Alana didn't know why she'd ever been so worried about announcing her pregnancy. From her coworkers to her parents, there was support all around. Sure, there were a few people who would judge and talk behind her back, but they were in the minority.

By and large, the people of Chatelaine were a good bunch.

That evening, Alana went next door to Mrs. Garcia's house to do a little light housekeeping. She dusted every Precious Moments figurine displayed, of which there were dozens. When she polished one that had obviously been glued back together, she counted the dents and scratches in the old ceramic paint and was reminded of her early days learning photography.

It was one of the only times a teacher had praised her. "You see things in a way no one else does."

She always got good grades in that class. She'd mastered composition. Lighting. Sometimes you worked with a model, and sometimes you worked with what you had. So much of art was arranging the piece to be seen in its best possible frame. If there were imperfections, you didn't show them. You turned to the unbroken side and showed the best, neglecting the cracks.

Because there were few things in life that were perfect. No perfect parents. No perfect children, either. No perfect love.

"Look what I got you today." From her recliner, where she sat with Luigi, her tabby cat, Mrs. Garcia held up a package of diapers, "They were on sale when my son took me for my weekly shopping."

"You didn't have to do that."

"Well, honey, no offense, but you young'uns don't always know where and how to find a bargain." She tapped her chest. "You can count on me for that."

Alana was unfortunately well acquainted with bargain hunting, such as the cheapest labels and using free shipping discounts, but she let Mrs. Garcia believe otherwise. She simply wanted to help.

"Thank you. This is so kind."

"And also, your feller was over here earlier."

Wait. What? Coop was here? Today?

"Who? You mean Coop?"

"That nice young man I've seen you with lately. The one who came to pick you up. My eyes aren't what they used to be, but I'm sure it was him. I heard him knocking, and when I came to the window, I caught him peeking inside. He waved and left when he realized you weren't home and that I was watching him. Did he catch up with you later?"

"No. I wonder what he wanted."

Possibly one last roll in the sheets for old times' sake before they broke it off for good?

*Damn it, stop thinking that's all men want from you.*

*Stop thinking it's all you have to give.*

"My eyesight might be going, honey, but that is one good-looking cowboy. He's rugged. Masculine.

Handsome but not pretty, you know? I imagine the ladies are all after him."

*They will be now.*

The thought of him with anyone else made her chest squeeze with a terrible ache. One disadvantage of staying in Chatelaine would be having to get used to seeing him with another woman, and probably soon. Coop wasn't the type to be single for long. In the past she hadn't been, either, but she'd changed. She no longer wanted a relationship for the sake of having one. For fear of winding up alone.

Because she *wasn't* alone and maybe never had been.

She had her parents, Mrs. Garcia, Lucy, Remi, Linc, Sari, Paul and so many of the customers she'd come to know by name. She had Coop, too—as a friend, of course.

It took a village, and she just might have her village right here in Chatelaine.

Sometimes, she wondered if she might have been hasty in saying no to Coop's marriage suggestion. While she'd never seemed to ask for enough from old boyfriends, maybe she'd mistakenly overshot this time. She'd reached for the stars. Maybe this time she'd asked for *too* much. Love and marriage, hand in hand, just like her parents. Because she'd said no, now she didn't even have Coop to keep her warm at night. To go with her to the ultrasounds and hold her hand. She should have figured out a way to keep him. She should have swallowed her pride and said yes.

*Sure, yes, I'll marry you. You can grow to love me the way I love you. Maybe.*

But it was her heart speaking now. She had to be smarter.

Alana's landline was ringing when she walked inside her home, and she rushed to pick it up.

"May I speak to Alana Searle, please?" The unfamiliar voice of a woman came over the phone.

"This is she."

"Hi, there. This is Justine Mendoza, formerly Justine Fortune Maloney. I know we haven't met, but I've heard so much about you."

Coop's sister? Alana had no idea why Justine was calling her. What could she possibly want? Still, she had to admit, she was intrigued. "You have?"

"Coop told me everything you've been experiencing. You probably know I went through the same thing."

Ah, the pregnancy. "Yes, he mentioned that. I'm glad to hear it worked out so well for you and your husband."

"It's not like it was easy, but gosh, little Morgan is worth it. There's not a single day I regret having him, even if he wasn't planned. And I was ready to do this all on my own, though it didn't help that my mother wasn't supportive. I felt all alone. Plus, I didn't want Stefan to marry me simply out of a sense of honor And that's all it was in the beginning, or at least, I thought so."

Had Coop called Justine after the failed proposal?

"Um, did Coop talk to you?"

"Yes, sometime last week or so. Why?"

So, Justine didn't know.

"Well, two days ago, Coop proposed to me."

Dead silence on the other end of the line. She was getting tired of leaving people speechless.

"Hello?"

"I'm still here," Justine replied. "Just…shocked. But I guess I'm not surprised. He mentioned I might want to call you sometime and give you advice. Support. It sounded like you two had just started dating and he wanted to help."

"That's how it started. He's been good to me."

"And you two fell in love?"

This time Alana was the silent one, but only for a beat. "Well, *I* did."

"Should I say congratulations?"

"I said no."

"Ah. Let me guess. You think Coop only asked you to marry him out of a sense of honor. Trying to step up and do the right thing when the real father didn't."

"Yes."

"And because you love him, you want more. You want the real thing."

Justine had the situation nailed. Before, Alana might have married Patrick if he'd asked her. She hadn't been as invested in him because she didn't love him. But with Coop, she would never settle for less than everything.

"Am I crazy?"

"Of course not. You deserve to be loved and adored. You should be with a man who's totally and completely and madly in love. Don't settle for less than you deserve."

"I did the right thing, even if it hurts."

"For what it's worth, I know my brother. And I'm here to tell you, if he doesn't want to do something, he just won't. He couldn't be forced on pain of death to do anything he doesn't want to do. Everyone says he's a daredevil who will take every risk, but that's not true. I've seen him walk away before. He's never been someone to cave to peer pressure. If it's not his decision, he won't do it. He might really love you, Alana, even if he didn't say so." She took a deep breath. "And I take it he didn't."

"No. It really wasn't the most romantic of proposals, to tell the truth. More like a suggestion."

Justine snorted. "That's my brother. But if he were to ask again, with all the bells and whistles, what would you say?"

"I don't think he will. Maybe I blew my only chance."

"But if he does?"

Alana pictured Coop, and her heart knew the answer. His wicked smile. The way he'd come over to take care of her without question. The night they'd danced under the stars in front of his truck.

She didn't think they'd ever have a dull moment together in an entire lifetime.

The next night, Alana went over to Sari's for dinner with her and the boys. It was such a sweet gesture, and Alana appreciated it now more than ever. The invite had come at the right time. She'd already cleaned house, done her laundry and spent time uploading some of her newer photos, playing with filters and editing them.

Her nights would be empty without Coop, so she had to find ways to fill them. She missed the way he'd braced himself above her, smiling so wickedly, kissing her until she was on fire. The nights they'd spent together, he would get up and bring her a glass of water if she was thirsty. And he was the only man she'd ever met who didn't mind cuddling after making love.

Now that she'd be on her own, whether here or in San Diego, Alana figured she better have a trial by fire. She'd see firsthand the life of a single mom. Sari was also doing it on her own, living in a twelve-unit apartment complex. Her husband had passed away at thirty-two of a heart attack, her parents had already passed away and she had no siblings, either. So she was truly on her own. Just her and the boys.

Benjy and Jacob were adorable redheads, practically the image of their mother. Both were dressed in adorable matching red-and-white pajama sets with a pattern of trains rolling across the tracks.

"Hi." Jacob, the two-year-old, hid behind his mother and peeked around her leg.

"Hello, Jacob." Alana bent low to meet his eyes. "I've heard so much about you."

"What about me?" Benjy piped up. "Did Mommy tell you about me?"

"I know you're Benjy." Alana straightened. "She told me you're a *big* helper."

"Yes, he's my little man of the house." Sari ruffled the four-year-old's hair.

"Yesterday, I chased a fly outside with a swatter," Benjy said proudly. "They don't belong inside. Right, Mommy?"

Sari chuckled and picked up a clingy Jacob. "That's right. Let's go into the kitchen and have dinner with our guest."

"We worked really hard," Benjy said. "I cleaned up all my toys."

"Me, too!" said Jacob. "I helped."

"Since we moved to Chatelaine, we haven't had any guests, so you're pretty much our first," Sari said.

"I'm honored."

The kids were amazingly well behaved through dinner, which was a delicious vegetable lasagna.

Alana saw proof that toddlers would indeed eat their vegetables. Sari really was a bit of a health nut, but she'd confessed to hiding vegetables in sauces just to get the required daily allowances for her boys. There was no sugar on the menu, and dessert was fresh pineapple and kiwi with yogurt. The kids lapped it up like it was ice cream.

Sari marched them to brush their teeth, then all four sat together and watched a Disney movie. Jacob cuddled in his mother's arms and was asleep after an hour.

"I'm too big to cuddle," Benjy said proudly.

"No, you're not," Sari said and kissed his cheek.

"But I don't fall asleep in the middle of the movie."

In fact, he lasted nearly to the end and then rested his head in Sari's lap and was down for the count in no time. It was all so cozy, their little family. A father was missing, but they still had each other.

"Would you take Jacob from me?" Sari asked. "I'll take Benjy. He's a lot heavier."

Alana took the younger boy, who nestled into her arms and sighed. She laid him down in the race car toddler bed next to Benjy's.

"I had them bathed and in their pj's early so I could shorten the bedtime routine tonight. Normally, we eat, then have bath time and reading. We rarely watch movies. It's a special treat."

Sari kissed each of her sons lightly on the forehead, shut the lights off and beckoned for Alana to follow her out of the room. In the kitchen she used a step stool and reached to a top cabinet, where she pulled out a GreatStore bag.

It was filled with chocolate bars.

"Don't judge. This is my personal weakness." Sari offered one to Alana. "Coconut and dark chocolate. I allow myself one every month or so."

Alana unwrapped her chocolate bar. "I never thought a single mom's life could be like this. You three are a perfect little family. The boys adore you, and you manage so well on your own."

"Don't let tonight fool you. They were on their best behavior. I bribed them and said they could watch a movie tonight if they were good."

"They're little angels." She followed Sari into the living room.

"Well, I think so, most of the time." She took a seat on the couch and unwrapped the candy bar. "But it's not easy. There's no one to back me up when I make a rule. No one to play good cop, bad cop with me. If I need medicine at night for one of the boys, I have to take them with me—there's no one to run out and bring it back. And if I should ever get too sick to function in the middle of the night, I'm not sure what we would do. Thank goodness I rarely get sick."

"I never thought of that. Please call me next time you need someone. I can run out and get the medicine."

Sari thanked her. "I'm making friends in town. My next-door neighbor is someone I would likely call in an emergency."

Unfortunately, Alana wouldn't be able to rely on Mrs. Garcia for much of anything.

"I wanted to have you over tonight so we could talk privately, out of the ears of other GreatStore employees."

"By now, I think everyone knows." Alana patted her belly.

"How are your parents handling the news? You told them?"

Finally, Alana could share that she had. "Yes. I broke down and told them just the other night."

"And?"

"Well, there were plenty of tears on both sides. But you were right, I'm glad I told them. They're supportive. So much so, they want me to move to San Diego with them. They'll be close by, even if I don't live with them. I know their support would be invaluable."

"Oh." Sari gaped. "I would miss you, but I guess that's not too surprising."

"I wanted to stay here in Chatelaine, but…well,

things haven't worked out too well with me and Coop. We broke up."

Sari reached for Alana's hand and squeezed it. "I'm sorry. I thought maybe you'd found yourself a good one."

Oh, he was a good one. He just didn't give her everything she needed. Like love. "He suggested we get married. Coop is such a sweetheart, and he wants to help. We get along in so many ways. Sometimes I feel like I know him better than I know myself. He likes me, I know, but that's not enough for a marriage."

Sari waved her hands. "Did I hear you right? He asked you to *marry* him?"

"No, he didn't *ask*. It was almost as if he'd just come up with the idea on the fly—'Hey, why don't we do this? You need a baby daddy. I need a warm body in my bed every night.'" She felt her cheeks heat up. "As I said, we get along very well."

Sari quirked a brow. "A man doesn't offer marriage just to have regular conjugal visits."

"Maybe that's true, but I'm not marrying someone who simply wants to take care of me. I want what my parents have. You should see them together. No one can infiltrate their world. As a kid, it made me feel ignored sometimes so I stupidly acted out. They used to embarrass the heck out of me, but now I just want a relationship like theirs. They were my example of healthy romantic love.

No, they weren't perfect parents but who is, anyway? They did something right if they showed me what real love looks like. It's not about sex like I used to think, but about always being there for each other. Putting each other first like they always did."

"You're lucky." A wistful look crossed Sari's gaze. "My husband and I were like that."

"Then you were lucky, too."

Sari nodded. "I understand if you don't want to settle for someone who doesn't love you, but if you love him…well, doesn't that count for something?"

"How do you know I love him?"

"Because you're hurt he didn't offer you a real proposal. You're hurt because you think marriage was only a suggestion because of your situation."

"That's not it at all. He said he cared about me. *Cared.*"

"You know what? In the beginning, I wasn't entirely sure my husband loved me nearly as much as I loved him. Later, there were other times when I suspected he loved me more than I loved him. But we grew into our love until we were like the branches of a tree, stronger together than we ever were apart. Now, I'd give anything for one more day with him." Sari's eyes grew misty. "Don't ever give up on someone you love. Give Coop time to come around, to realize that he loves you. Because, unless he's some strange mythical creature, he would not have suggested marriage without some strong feelings for you. Whether he can put the right words to those feelings or not."

Justine had said something similar about Coop. She'd also said that he couldn't be forced to do anything he didn't already want to do. And that he might really love Alana if he'd gone as far as suggesting marriage.

The thought made her heart lift for the first time since she'd broken things off with Coop.

Marriage to the man she loved. A healthy child.

Even now, it seemed too much to hope for.

## Chapter Sixteen

Coop was about to do something either very stupid or incredibly smart.

For the second time this month, he waltzed into the bar where Damon worked. Most of the time, Coop considered the Chatelaine Bar and Grill to be out of his price range. He drank cold beer at home. Occasionally, at the end of a long day with the other ranch hands, he drank it clear out of someone's ice chest. The poor man's bar. But he had to stop thinking of himself as a *poor* man and start thinking like a wealthy one. He'd have that Fortune inheritance, and it no longer mattered when it came. It would arrive, and that was the important thing. He *wasn't* any less deserving than his siblings.

"Hey." Coop plunked himself on an empty stool at the end of the bar.

Damon grinned and reached for a beer, which he uncapped and set in front of Coop. "A popular IPA. Enjoy."

"Thanks." Coop took a big pull and set it down. "I need some advice."

"About?" Damon crossed his arms. "Don't tell me you're still after Alana. Move on, dude. Check me out. Since that bachelor auction, I've had two crushes and gotten over them."

"That was quick."

"That's why it's called a crush. You gotta be quick on your feet." He snapped his fingers.

"I have more than a crush on her. It turns out…" Coop busied himself with the label on the bottle, using his thumb to pull at the edge. "I'm in love."

Damon gaped. "Speaking of *quick*."

"It just happened, okay? I didn't plan on it. I was supposed to have a good old time and instead— If you make fun of me, I'll kill you. Instead…" Coop gripped the bottle nearly tight enough for it to break. "I'm going to ask her to marry me."

This time, he would ask. This time, it would be a big production. A real proposal. This time, maybe she'd say yes.

"Are you out of your mind?" Damon clutched his chest. "Why would you want *my* advice? I'll just tell you to forget her and run for the hills. If you leave now, you might make it to San Antonio before nightfall."

"I don't want to run. And I want *your* advice because—" Coop nearly choked on his next words. "Because you have more game than I do."

"Sorry?" Damon leaned forward, cupping a hand over his ear. "I don't think I heard you."

"You heard me." Coop may have growled. "I said you have more game than I do. Women love you. All women. Even the Silver Ladies. What's your damn secret?"

Damon chuckled and crossed his arms. "There's no secret. I love them first, and when women feel loved, it's like catnip to a cat."

"Elaborate."

"Well, son, it isn't just about the kissing and ca-noodling. Words matter. Women need the words."

"Good. I have words. What kind of words? Are you talking about how great her hair smells or what she's wearin'? Or are we talkin' dirty talk?"

Damon covered his face with his hands. "It's like I'm speaking to a toddler," he mumbled. Then he lowered his hands and studied Coop with a sharp gaze. "Haven't you ever told a woman you loved her?"

"Besides Mom?"

"Um, yeah, dude. She doesn't count."

He'd never said those words to a woman be-cause until now, he'd always doubted himself when it came to love. He would have called those emotions lust more than anything else, and because of what his own mother had been through, he'd been careful not to hurt any woman. Saying the words would cost him. They would bind him to a future he wasn't sure he wanted. But he wasn't an idiot. Clearly, he'd have to tell Alana he loved her, and he had no doubt it was true.

He couldn't go back to the person he'd been before her, nor did he want to. She'd changed him to be a better man without even trying. It was in her sweetness, in the way she liked everyone even when they were less than kind to her. She really didn't know how special and perfect she was and he'd love to spend the rest of his life reminding her. Yes, he loved her.

Those words were going to cost him this time, but only if he *didn't* say them.

Coop nodded. "Got it. I'll put into words what I've been trying to show her. But I also need a romantic gesture."

"A grand gesture, you mean?" Damon got busy and gave the bar a wipe.

"Why does everybody know what that is besides me?"

A couple of guys Coop recognized as GreatStore staff had not-so-discreetly been listening in, looking away only when Coop shot them a glare. Now they looked up.

"Chick flicks," one of them said.

"Man, I love chick flicks. They get me laid every time," said another.

Damon waved a hand dismissively. "Okay, no more comments from you bozos. My brother has real problems over here."

"No, I'm serious," the first guy said. "I think I've watched all the movies. *An Officer and a Gentleman, 10 Things I Hate About You, Pretty Woman*. You name it, I've seen it. Hey, do you own one of those old-fashioned boom boxes like our parents used to play?"

Coop squinted. "No."

"Never mind. That's a terrible idea," Damon said. "John Cusack won't work for everybody."

Slowly, the men inched closer toward Coop. "Do you happen to have access to a small airplane or a hot-air balloon?" one of them asked.

"Are you out of your mind?" Coop said.

"How big of a grand gesture do you want?" the second guy asked. "Keep in mind you can never really go *too* big."

"How about something between a boom box and a hot-air balloon?" Coop muttered.

Within minutes, a small crowd of men had gathered around them, talking rom-coms, chick flicks and grand gestures. Someone wrote on a napkin, drawing a chart with all options in order from practical to expensive.

"Aren't your brothers filthy rich? I'm sure they could get you a plane that would fly a banner reading whatever you want it to read."

Coop quirked a brow. "I'm not going to ask Linc or Max to rent a plane. This should come from me, and from the heart. Or am I missing something here?"

"You're missing nothing." Damon gestured to him. "Follow that train of thought."

"Can you sing?" one guy asked, looking up from his paper-napkin graph.

Others began shouting out suggestions.

"Is there any way you can arrange for her to be near a fire escape, then you rent a limo?"

"And bring flowers!"

"Are the two of you going to be in a public place where you can grab a microphone?"

"Does she have a younger sister you can do something really nice for?"

The guys argued with each other over whether every man should at some point learn how to sing.

One man let out a whistle to hush the crowd and offered a suggestion. "Shouldn't it rain again soon? You could stand out in the rain like a gall-darn fool and tell her you love her. Works like a charm."

Those words brought him back to the time he'd run over to Alana's in the last downpour and found her flat on her back after having slipped on her rain-slick floor. She'd been trying to protect her baby, worried if she moved, she might do damage. Looking so vulnerable that his heart had cracked wide-open. That night, they'd revealed secrets to each other. Deeply personal ones. He'd never told anyone else about his father until that night. Because of the gentle way she'd reacted, Coop had then had the courage to tell Linc what he'd held back for years.

And now he saw it all in a different light.

He thought about their first night together, when Alana had boldly won him at the auction. How reticent she'd been only a month later, until he figured out why. She'd given him plenty of clues that very night, ones that he only now recognized in hindsight. The baby would be her anchor and had already changed her. Steadied her. But change wasn't always bad, and in her case, it made her the woman Coop had fallen for, and hard.

Suddenly he knew exactly what to do. This would be special. Personal. Only Alana would understand this gesture, and hopefully, she'd always remember the moment.

"See you later!" He rushed out of the bar, leaving Damon and the guys still arguing.

"I think we can remove this dressing room and have the space we need." Paul pointed to the future site of *Your Kids and Your Pets*, a photo studio inside GreatStore.

It turned out the powers that be loved the idea,

thought it might bring in more business, and they would allocate funds for the equipment required. They only wanted a space to be found, one that wouldn't take away any of their current sales floor.

Alana still couldn't believe this was finally going to happen.

"It's true not many people use changing rooms anymore," said Sari, who was there to help with creative ideas. "We have such a great exchange policy I usually go home and try on the clothes. If they don't fit right, I can return them the next day."

Since Alana was a bit anal when it came to cleanliness, she'd stayed away from dressing rooms since the day she found someone's discarded panties on the floor. She'd begun to wonder exactly what on earth people were doing in the changing rooms. Remi swore it was just an attempt to shoplift a package of new panties by wearing them all at once, but good Lord, why leave the old ones where everyone could see?

"The location is perfect," Sari said with a big grin. "Sign me and my boys up to be your first customers."

Alana hugged her friend. "I can't wait."

It had been a week since she'd seen Coop, and the wave of sadness and regret hadn't ebbed. Some days it came in a big splash that threatened to take her under, while on others it was a tiny ripple of pain she could push back. Alana was busying herself with planning her future. Her parents would be visiting next month, no doubt mounting a full-frontal attack on why Alana should move to San Diego.

After speaking with Paul a bit longer, Alana clocked in and went to work behind the deli counter. The photos of food she'd posted on Instagram had brought in several customers a day, and Paul figured Alana was good for sales, so he'd kept her here another week. Honestly, now that she was past all the nausea of her first trimester, she didn't mind being around food. She'd been doing a fair amount of taste testing during downtimes.

A few minutes later, Mrs. DeWitt, one of her regular customers, had just ordered a pound of smoked turkey and a carton of potato salad when a voice squawked over the rarely used intercom.

"Your attention, please," Paul's voice rang out.

Oh, jeez. Alana winced, hoping Paul hadn't taken to announcing employee of the month this way. He'd dropped hints that she'd been selected once more, and she hoped he wasn't doing this to make her feel better. Paul had been going out of his way to try to cheer her up, assuring her he'd put her down on the wait list for the company's daycare center and that a raise was surely coming.

"One of our customers would like a few words," Paul said.

"A customer?" Mrs. DeWitt said. "Since when are *we* allowed…"

Another male voice, one Alana recognized far too well, spoke next. "I can't sing, folks, so I won't be. You're welcome."

Every clerk and customer had stopped what they were doing and was listening with rapt attention. Alana's gloved hand was poised over the scale, holding the sliced turkey, suspended in midair.

"But I still wanted to do something special for the woman I love. Something memorable. Um, it's called a grand gesture."

Alana's hand shook so badly she dropped the turkey on the scale.

"The first time I danced to this song, I didn't really understand it. Now, I do."

In the next moment, "Make You Miss Me" by Sam Hunt came blaring through the speakers.

One of the first songs she and Coop had ever danced to, in the dark, on their very first date. He'd made fun of that song and the heartbreak the song-writer had obviously experienced when he wrote it.

She could almost feel the heat of the truck's headlights on her skin and smell the lake water, fresh and still. It was supposed to be one date. Never would she have dreamed she'd fall in love this hard and fast. But this song was now a memory forever tied to Cooper Fortune Maloney. The man she'd love for the rest of her life.

Mrs. DeWitt covered her ears. "I thought we voted on this. Music. Too. *Loud.*"

The song played to its end, and then there stood Coop on the other side of the glass partition. She'd missed him so much the sight of him now brought fresh tears to her eyes.

"Hi, Coop," she said softly.

Mrs. DeWitt moved out of the way, and Coop came closer.

"Are you here for the specials?" Alana sniffed.

It was a joke, and a pathetic one. Everyone, both staff and customers, was staring, and she wanted to insert a little levity in the mix. She wasn't used to being the center of attention. Not like this.

He shook his head. "I want to ask you a question."

"Will this take long?" Mrs. DeWitt asked. "Because I was buying a pound of turkey."

"It's on me." Coop turned to her with a smile. "How about five pounds?"

"Well, you can certainly afford it," she muttered.

"Ask the question!" This was from Sari, as she smiled from the aisle, clutching dresses on hangers. "I have to get back to work, but I can't miss this."

"Excuse me," Coop said to Mrs. DeWitt, who took several more steps back. He sidled up to the glass case. "Sweetheart, I have something for you."

Alana felt as though she was having an out-of-body experience as he pulled a tiny box from his pocket.

Her skin tightened at the sight of the black jewelry box.

"It's not a ring," he whispered. "Because I want you to pick that out. I also want it to be the biggest bling you'd ever want, so you might have to wait a little while."

He handed over the box, and she opened it to find a sterling silver necklace with a charm. An anchor. It was breathtaking, so shiny and beautiful. She had no words.

Coop had somehow given her the perfect gift. Yes, even better than a ring. Because this told her he remembered. Her heart tugged and swelled.

"Remember what you said to me on our first date?" Coop asked her. "You said you used to be like me, but then you had an anchor that changed everything. At first, I didn't understand. Why would you want an anchor tying you down?"

"I remember."

"You tried to explain, but I still didn't understand. Maybe I'm a little slow, but I get it now. The baby is your anchor, but, Alana, you're mine. And you're right—this doesn't feel like a weight, or anything that would ever hold me back. It feels like I'm home and I want to stay."

Mrs. DeWitt pulled out a tissue and sniffed into it. "That's beautiful, son. You can forget about the turkey."

A crowd had gathered behind Coop. And in that group, Alana recognized Linc and Remi, Max and Eliza—even Lucy was here, holding a squirming little Uma. And an older woman Alana immediately recognized. She had the same earnest brown eyes as her son.

"Oh, yeah. I'm sure you remember my mother." Coop chuckled and gestured toward Kimberly Maloncy.

"Hello, Mrs. Maloney," Alana said. "Nice to see you again."

"I meant to have you over for dinner," Kimberly said. "But there hasn't been any time."

"Sorry, our courtship was fast," Cooper said. "Even for me."

"That's how it happens sometimes," Kimberly said with a smile and a nod of approval.

Coop turned to Alana and dropped to one knee. "Alana Searle, I love you with all my heart. Would you please marry me?"

There was a collective "aw" from the crowd, and Alana thought her heart would surely burst into a thousand pieces, she was so happy. She ran to the other side of the deli counter and straight into his arms.

"Yes! I love you so much. All I wanted was to hear you love me, too. I would *love* to marry you."

He smiled, and she fell a little bit more in love. If they were anything like her parents, and she believed they would be, they'd fall a little bit more in love every day.

*Proposed to at the deli counter.*

Well, Coop certainly was an original.

"Sweetheart, I know I'm not the best prospect for a father to your baby—"

"That's debatable," his mother interrupted.

Coop laughed. "Thanks, Mom." He turned back to Alana. "But I want to learn."

"Coop, I'm going to be learning, too. Who says I'm going to be the best mother? All any parent can do is love their baby with all their heart. And try."

"We'll learn together," Coop said.

Paul's voice rang out from the crowd. "Folks, this is the first official GreatStore marriage proposal. We like to say we're like a little family here, and today that's especially true."

Alana couldn't help but laugh. "Yes, but we're not getting married in aisle nine," she said.

"Vegas?" Lucy called out. "That sounds like you, Coop. You, too, Alana. Make it quick and flashy."

"Nah," Coop said. "I want to take my time and do this right. A big wedding right here in Chatelaine with all our family and friends. What do you say, future bride?"

"As you wish."

## Chapter Seventeen

"Are you ready for this?" Coop squeezed Alana's hand.

They sat in his truck at the end of the circular driveway to Linc's house.

"You mean this is all for us?" She looked wide-eyed at the cars lining both sides of the street, caterers carrying in trays of food. "My parents are going to be so surprised."

They'd flown in the week after Coop's proposal, and his mother had invited everyone over for a big family dinner.

"Linc said he wanted to throw us a big engagement party. You know my brother—he's a generous guy. And you love a party as much as I do. Let's go have fun."

She smiled and reached out to frame his face. "I love you."

"I love you, darlin'. Now, let's go have us an engagement party."

It had only been two weeks since he'd asked Alana to marry him, and word had spread through Chatelaine like wildfire, since it had been a bit of a public proposal in the first place. People were talking, that was for sure.

*"I always thought they were like two peas in a pod."*

*"How about that? It turns out he had a thing for her all along. Who knew?"*

*"They're having a big wedding, I heard. I hope to get an invite."*

Coop had heard it all by now. He'd invite the whole town to the shebang, if he could, but he still didn't even have a ring for Alana. They'd already been to the jeweler, where Alana had picked out a few rings she liked. For now, she wore the sterling silver anchor pendant around her neck and refused to take it off.

But she'd teased him about the lack of a ring every morning, singing Beyoncé's song and reminding him he hadn't put a ring on it. She claimed she'd just as soon him get her a plastic ring from the gumball machines at GreatStore. But hell no—he'd learned his lesson when it came to grand gestures. His woman was going to have the best there was, and he couldn't wait for his inheritance so he could buy it for her.

On the fifth morning of her relentless teasing, he'd rolled out of bed and gone into the kitchen, having come up with a solution.

"Give me that finger," he'd said, reentering the bedroom.

She'd quirked a brow and come up on her elbow, smiling. "You haven't had time to run to the store and use the gumball machine. What's up?"

"It's my other interim solution."

He'd then tied a thick band of twine around her finger several times, then brought her hand up to his lips and kissed it. "No one will question you're mine now."

"Aw, Coop. You roped me."

"Better than a gumball machine. And when that check comes, you're getting the biggest piece of bling there is."

"You are *such* a romantic." She kissed him and took him back to bed.

Now, he was moments away from celebrating his engagement to the most beautiful woman in the world.

Inside, they met up with the rest of the family. Alana's parents were already there, and so was his mother. Max and Eliza, who'd come down from San Antonio for the weekend to celebrate with them.

Damon, even Justine, Stefan and little Morgan had driven down from Rambling Rose.

"Go say hi to Uncle Coop," Justine bent to say to her little boy.

Morgan gazed up at her with the adoring look only a small boy could give to his mother. Then he toddled over to Coop, a drooly smile on his face, and held up his arms.

"Hey, little man." Coop picked him up. "Morgan, meet Alana. Soon enough you're going to have a little cousin to chase around."

"Hi, Morgan," Alana said, running the back of her hand across his cheek. "I've heard a lot about you."

"Cooscoo," said Morgan, as if this was his way of greeting someone. Having done his duty, he squirmed to be put down, then ran back to his mother.

"Hey, bro." Linc appeared at Coop's side. "Congratulations again to both of you."

"You went all out," Coop said. "Thank you."

"Nothing but the best for you." Linc clapped him on the back. "I can't believe we both got engaged about the same time. We'll see who has the first wedding. Remi and I might just beat you two to the altar. Congratulations on catching him, Alana."

"Well, there's some argument as to who caught whom." He brought his and Alana's hands together and brushed a kiss across her knuckles. "Hey, I might be a risk-taker, but I'm also wicked smart. I roped her before she could get away."

A fancy waiter was passing around trays of hors d'oeuvres. Another was behind the bar in the living room mixing up drinks, flutes of sparkling wine already poured and ready for any takers. Coop was brought back to the night of the auction and the first time he'd ever spent any serious time talking to Alana. To think she'd been right here in Chatelaine all along, and he'd nearly missed her. The thought never failed to unnerve him.

"Congratulations." Alana's father shook Coop's hand. "You've got a good one there."

"Don't I know it, sir. Thank you."

Alana and her mother embraced, then he and Alana made the rounds, holding hands as they made their way to mingle with everyone who'd showed up to celebrate.

"Lunch is being served on the patio in about ten minutes," Remi announced.

When Coop and Alana split for a moment, her wanting to hit the bathroom, he wandered into the library he'd heard so much about. Floor-to-ceiling shelves of books, just as Alana had described. It was an open room, with a big picture window letting in streams of bright sunlight.

Coop turned, and nearby in a chair sat Martin Smith, nursing a flute of sparkling wine. His gray hair was neatly combed, his beard grizzled.

"Hello, young man. I was just sitting here alone and admiring these works of art. Print books. Don't you know, someday every one of them will be considered a rarity, I fear." The elderly man stood and offered his hand. "I understand congratulations are in order."

A little unnerved by finding the man at his engagement party, Coop just nodded and shook his hand.

"Oh, don't look so shocked. I was invited." Martin chuckled. "Which is rather convenient for me, because I was planning to come by soon and pay you a visit anyway."

Coop held his body very still. This could be the moment his entire life would change course.

"Coop?" Alana called from the hallway.

"Right in here, baby." He beckoned to her. She should be here with him at this life-changing occasion.

She wandered in and came to his side.

"Martin, have you met my fiancée?" Coop put his arm around Alana and made the introductions.

"Lovely to meet you, dear. Congratulations on your engagement." Martin fished in his pocket and presented Coop with a check. "And I'm truly sorry for the delay."

Coop stared at a check with more zeros than he'd thought he'd ever see in his lifetime. "Um, thank you, Martin."

"No need to thank *me*." He pressed a hand to his chest. "I'm just the deliveryman. For what it's worth, I know your grandfather Wendell Fortune would be very proud of you today."

"Thank you, that's good to hear."

Coop wondered if Martin had heard Coop was marrying Alana even though she was pregnant with another man's child. For Coop's part, he liked to pretend the baby was his, and for all practical purposes, Alana assured him the baby would be his son. *His son.* He'd do a lot better for him than Rick Maloney had ever done for any of his sons.

"I'm sure you'll spend the money in a good place." Martin glanced over to Alana, smiled, then made his way past them.

Alana threw her arms around him. "See, I told you! Coop, I'm so happy for you!"

"For *us*." Coop bent low to kiss her. "You, me and our baby."

Max joined them in the library a few moments later, and his neck jerked back when he saw what Coop held in his hand.

"Is this what I think it is?" he asked.

Coop held up the check with all the zeros. "Yep. My inheritance."

"All right, dude!"

Max gave Coop a manly hug, then hugged Alana. "Welcome to the family. Maybe you're Coop's good-luck charm."

"Max," Coop asked, "don't you think the timing is a little odd? I mean, we get engaged, and next thing you know, I have my inheritance check."

"It's almost like old Grandpa Wendell is listening from beyond the grave." Max chuckled.

Linc appeared in the doorway. "What's up? What are you all doing in Remi's library? We're about to sit down and eat."

"Guess who just got his check from Martin Smith?" Max grinned.

"You're kidding!" Lincoln strode into the room. "That's fantastic. Best news I've had all week."

"What's the first thing you're going to do with that check, bro?" Max said.

"Take her to the jewelry store," Coop answered, holding up Alana's roped ring finger. "To get her the big bauble she picked out so everyone will know she's mine."

"That's not what I would have guessed you'd do first," Max said. "You were the one who told Linc to go spend his money in Las Vegas, *The Hangover* style."

Cooper winced at the memory. So much had changed for him in a short time. He had a better perspective of what mattered. Good thing he hadn't received this check any sooner. Timing was everything.

"Well, after the jewelry store, what's next?" Linc tipped back on his heels. "Even I had a big party."

"I'm sure we'll have one at some point." Coop slid a smile to Alana. "Probably our wedding reception. But first, I'm getting Alana a safe vehicle, not that little death trap she drives. I'll need a new truck, too, one with more than two seats. And I want to look at ranches. One with plenty of land, but a house big enough for the baby to have a nursery and whatever else he might need."

"We should have lots of bedrooms for our future children, too," Alana piped up.

"And I want a separate photo studio for Alana. Like a shed. A she-shed."

"Oh, Coop. That's not—"

"Absolutely, sweetheart. It's important. My passion is horses, and I think you should continue with your photography. You love that and are too good to give it up. The GreatStore gig is a start, but maybe you can even open your own studio someday."

"Eliza has recommended you to a Realtor in Chatelaine. I'll email you his information," Max said.

"Sounds good." Taking Alana's hand, Coop led them out of the library. "C'mon, let's go tell our parents the good news."

But when they walked into the living room, not surprisingly, they discovered Kimberly had already heard the news. Obviously so had Damon, who was dancing around like he'd caught the winning touchdown in the end zone, no doubt knowing he was one step closer to *his* check.

Kimberly enveloped Coop in a warm hug. "I told you, honey. Good things come to those who wait. You were patient, and you've been rewarded."

"You wouldn't believe what he's going to do with all the money, Mom." Max elbowed Coop.

She quirked a brow. "Take care of his family, I believe."

"How did you guess?" Linc said.

"I knew it the moment he proposed to Alana." Kimberly drew Alana into a hug. "That's what a good woman does to a man. Gives him perspective."

As usual, his mother was right.

This daredevil, out-of-control cowboy had settled down. Now he looked forward to spending the rest of his life on a ranch with Alana and their children.

\* \* \* \* \*

*Look for the next installment of the new continuity*
*The Fortunes of Texas: Hitting the Jackpot.*
*Don't miss*

**Fortune's Fatherhood Dare**
*by Makenna Lee*
*On sale April 2023, wherever Harlequin*
*books and ebooks are sold.*

*And don't miss the previous titles in*
*The Fortunes of Texas: Hitting the Jackpot*

**A Fortune's Windfall**
*by USA TODAY bestselling*
*author Michelle Major*

**Fortune's Dream House**
*by Nina Crespo*

*Available now!*

# COMING NEXT MONTH FROM

## HARLEQUIN®
## SPECIAL EDITION™

### #2971 FORTUNE'S FATHERHOOD DARE
*The Fortunes of Texas: Hitting the Jackpot* • by Makenna Lee
When bartender Damon Fortune Maloney boasts that he can handle any kid, single mom Sari Keeling dares him to watch her two rambunctious boys for just one day. It's game on, but Damon soon discovers that parenthood is tougher than he thought—and so is resisting Sari.

### #2972 HER MAN OF HONOR
*Love, Unveiled* • by Teri Wilson
Bridal-advice columnist and jilted bride Everly England couldn't have predicted the feelings a sympathetic kiss from her best friend would ignite in her. Henry Aston knows the glamorous city girl is terrified romance will ruin their friendship. But this stand-in groom plans to win her "I do" after all!

### #2973 MEETING HIS SECRET DAUGHTER
*Forever, Texas* • by Marie Ferrarella
When nurse Riley Robertson brought engineer Matt O'Brien to Forever to meet the daughter he never knew he had, she was only planning to help Matt see that he can be the father his little girl needs. But could the charming new dad be the man Riley didn't know she needed? And are the three ready to become a forever family?

### #2974 THE RANCHER'S BABY
*Aspen Creek Bachelors* • by Kathy Douglass
Suddenly named guardian of a baby girl, rancher Isaac Montgomery gamely steps up for daddy duty, with the help of new neighbor Savannah Rogers. Sparks fly, but Savannah's reserved even as their feelings heat up. Are Isaac and his baby too painful a reminder of her heartbreaking loss? Or do they hold the key to healing?

### #2975 ALL'S FAIR IN LOVE AND WINE
*Love in the Valley* • by Michele Dunaway
Unexpectedly back in town, Jack Clayton is acting as if he never crushed Sierra James's teenage heart. When he offers to buy her family's vineyard, the former navy lieutenant knows Jack is turning on the charm, but no way is she planning to melt for him again. But will denying what she still feels for Jack prove to be a victory she can savor?

### #2976 NO RINGS ATTACHED
*Once Upon a Wedding* • by Mona Shroff
Fleeing her own nuptials wasn't part of wedding planner Sangeeta Parikh's plan. Neither was stumbling into chef Sonny Pandya's arms and becoming an internet sensation! So why not fake a relationship so Sangeeta can save face and her job, and to get Sonny much-needed exposure for his restaurant? It's a good plan for two commitmentphobes...until their fake commitment starts to feel all too real.

---

**YOU CAN FIND MORE INFORMATION ON UPCOMING HARLEQUIN TITLES, FREE EXCERPTS AND MORE AT HARLEQUIN.COM.**

HSECNM0223

# HARLEQUIN
## PLUS

Try the best multimedia subscription service for romance readers like you!

---

## Read, Watch and Play.

Experience the easiest way to get the romance content you crave.

Start your **FREE TRIAL** at
www.harlequinplus.com/freetrial.